OWNING BEAUTY

A DARK MAFIA ARRANGED MARRIAGE ROMANCE

STELLA ANDREWS

Copyrighted Material
Copyright © Stella Andrews 2020
Stella Andrews has asserted her rights under the Copyright, Designs and Patents Act 1988 to be identified as the Author of this work. This book is a work of fiction and except in the case of historical fact, any resemblance to actual persons, living or dead, is purely coincidental.
All rights reserved. No part of this book may be reproduced or transmitted in any form without written permission of the author, except by a reviewer who may quote brief passages for review purposes only.

18+ This book is for Adults only. If you are easily shocked and not a fan of sexual content then move away now.

NEWSLETTER

Sign up to my newsletter and download a free book

stellaandrews.com

OWNING BEAUTY

**Hard. Dominant. Overbearing & Insufferable.
The man I agreed to marry.**

My biggest mistake has a name.

Tobias Moretti. *Tall, dark and dangerous and the head of the largest crime family this area has ever seen.*

Brooding, mysterious and so hot he melts the resolve of any woman he meets.

Did I mention he was rich? Then again, my billion-dollar inheritance may have something to do with the deal we just made.

Marry him and escape my hated past.

Play the trophy wife in public and then get on with my day – alone.

No other men and a life with everything I want - except love.

How can I miss what I never had in the first place?

At least I'd have my freedom – think again.

It turns out my freedom is the last thing I can have. Guarded by men in black suits and forbidden to go out alone.

A trapped bird in a cage filled with luxury.

Then it changes.

The terms of our contract have been re-written. He wants a wife in every sense of the word.

Yes, my biggest mistake wants it all. He wants to own my mind, body and soul and I don't get a say in the matter.

Tobias.

I like to own the best that money can buy.
I like to surround myself with beauty and Art.

I want the best and don't care how far I go to own it.

She's about to discover that I always go a step too far.

She gave up everything to be my wife but there is still one valuable asset she owns that causes the feral beast in me to growl.

Her innocence.

My world is a dark and dangerous place full of nightmares that never go away.

My beauty is about to wake up and discover the prince who rescued her from the tower is a beast in disguise and she will hear me roar as I claim the innocence of my virgin bride.

Yes, I can live without love but I can't live without that and nothing is going to stand in my way because what Tobias Moretti wants – he gets, over and over again.

CHAPTER 1

ANASTASIA

I see them coming. The sleek, dark cars, rolling into the drive, one behind the other, here to seal my fate. Powerful machines that hide their occupants from a world that would be a much better place without them in it.

I watch with morbid fascination as they come to a slow stop and the passenger doors on each individual car open. Identical men in black suits step into the light, shielding their eyes from the glare of the sun with the blackest shade.

There's a silent menace that surrounds them, and I shiver.

But they are not the ones here for me.

He is.

The man who has yet to show himself, but I know lurks inside the middle car like a King closely guarded by his minions.

My fiancé.

My heart beats so fast I'm sure he can hear it and can probably taste my fear because it's there, deep within me, growing by the second as I contemplate what a mistake I've just made.

I signed my life away to move from one prison to another.

"Anastasia, they're here, get your things."

I don't turn around because my mother no longer calls the shots. She gave up that right when she engineered this sham of a marriage.

"Did you hear me, hurry, we don't want to keep Mr. Moretti waiting."

I carry on watching from the window and he still doesn't emerge from the car. Can he see me? Of course he can. I expect it amuses him to see his caged bird waiting to swap one cage for another. He is probably reveling in the moment he gains another possession to add to his pile.

The men stand with their backs to the cars as if waiting for orders, and they probably are.

"Anastasia, I said, hurry up—now."

Mom's voice is high and panicked. She won't rest until I'm safely inside one of those black cars and out of her hair because I'm in no doubt she is scared. Any sane person would be when a monster comes calling. Not me, all I feel is curiosity.

She moves across and pulls my arm, and I stumble a little. In a tight, angry voice, she whispers, "Don't make me pull you out of here by your hair, you ungrateful child."

I have no tears to waste on this pathetic excuse for a mother, so I snatch my arm back angrily and snarl, "Tell him to come and get me."

"What?"

Mom's voice is shocked, and I smile inside. "Come and get you. Are you mad? Nobody asks Mr. Moretti to do anything, don't be a fool, Anastasia and just get your things and go, they're waiting."

"I said, tell him to come and get me."

I stare out of the window and take some pleasure in

picturing him inside his car, having to wait. I'm guessing he never has to wait. In fact, I'm surprised he's even here at all. He could have sent a car and carried on with his day. Maybe he has, but then again, I know he's there, watching me from behind the tinted glass, probably growing more irritated by the second and it amuses me to play with the last shred of power I hold.

So, I stare at the middle car and giggle inside as I'm tempted to give him my middle finger. Then again, how would that look? His new wife setting in place the tone of their relationship before it's even got off the ground.

"Anastasia, honey, please, don't make me ask him."

"Why?"

"Because it's not right. He may change his mind and then where would we be?"

I shrug. "We would be fine."

A gentle voice says softly, "Honey, are you ok?"

The tears prick like acid behind my eyes as the only woman I love inside these walls voices her concern. Martha, my former nanny, and now our housekeeper, enters the room.

"I'm fine." I inject a little warmth into my voice because she has earned it over the years. She's been more like a mother to Angel and me and deserves some respect. "Can you ask Mr. Moretti to come and collect my cases, please Martha?"

My mom's sharp intake of breath makes me smile inside and I can only imagine the look they share as Martha leaves the room as quietly as she entered it.

Mom hisses, "You always were a difficult child, there's no reasoning with you when you're in one of your moods. If this all goes wrong, it's your fault you ungrateful bitch."

Once again, I say nothing because I'm tired. Tired of trying to live up to her high expectations. Tired of trying to win her approval by allowing her to push me around and tired of life. Am I being difficult, hell yeah, because this is the last piece of control I have? After today I'll have none because Tobias Moretti will have what he wants, mom will have what she wants, and once again, it will be because I let them.

The door slams and I breathe a sigh of relief. She's gone.

Pressing my face to the window, I don't care if he sees me. He must know this isn't my choice, and yet he is still seeing it through. I'm not stupid, even though they all think I am. I fight the bitterness that's sat with me my whole life. Now I have something of value a man such as he wants, and this is the trade-off. Marry Tobias Moretti and he gains control of my shares in Johnson's plastics, a company formed by my father and now ran by my sister and her boyfriend Sebastian Stone - my former fiancé. Yes, life's a bitch and I had the misfortune to be raised by the biggest one of all. Mirabelle Johnson, widow of Harvey Johnson, a vile man whose only pleasure in life was making money and screwing around behind his wife's back. How ironic that his daughter will marry a man exactly like him because this marriage is an arrangement. A business deal that sets me free from my mom and free to live my own solitary life away from her.

I doubt I'll even see my husband much, which is fine by me because I don't even know the man. Only what I discovered when I stalked him online.

Tobias Moretti, tall, dark and dangerous and the head of the largest crime family this area has ever seen. He hides behind respectability, buying up failing businesses and turning them around. But it's well known that the real business he runs is underground. Nobody messes with the Moretti family—they would be a fool if they did. Which is why I feel the excitement building inside as I make the man himself wait and listen to my immature demands.

Martha walks across the drive toward the middle car and I see her talking urgently to one of the men in suits. I can only imagine her apologetic request, and my heart hardens. How dare they wait outside without even the courtesy of pretending to care for my feelings?

The man knocks on the window of the middle car and I watch the window lower and he leans down and speaks to the person inside. I hold my breath as my heart beats frantically inside and feel the excitement grip me as I picture his anger. Will he come? This will be interesting.

Then the man straightens up and I watch in disbelief as he reaches for the handle and the door opens. My mouth goes dry as a leg swings out, closely followed by a man dressed in a well-tailored suit. He looks up and our eyes meet across the distance, and there's no mistaking the power in those eyes. Two dark pools of danger defy the sun and stare right at me. The man they belong to makes my soul weep and my heart pound mercilessly inside me. *You're a fool.* My inner voice mocks me as I stare at the man I'm about to call my husband and I see the promise in those eyes.

As my heart beats furiously, my legs tremble and my breath hitches, I know that man is dangerous and now I'm in more trouble than I ever thought possible.

CHAPTER 2

ANASTASIA

*H*e walks to the door and I see my mom waiting there, almost bowing her apology. She stands to the side as he sweeps past her, closely followed by the man who stood outside his car. Turning away from the window, I question my own sanity as I wait to see what happens next and am almost tempted to hide under my bed until the monster goes away because I'm in no doubt at all, that man is the biggest monster around here and I've just angered him.

I hear footsteps on the staircase and swallow hard. In just three seconds he will be here. What have I done?

My mouth dries and I lick my lips in anticipation of our first meeting. What will he say - what will I say? I would be a fool to say anything at all, but at this moment, I feel more alive than I have ever felt before. What will happen?

There's a gentle knock on the door and I try to inject some power in my voice and say, "The door is open."

As it opens, I set my face to my usual blank expression and look with morbid curiosity as the monster enters the tower.

"Anastasia."

His voice is deep and slightly husky, and the man that stands in my doorway fills it with an authority that is hard to ignore. My breath hitches as I take my first look at the man I have only seen on the screen, and I almost take a step back as I feel the full force of him. It's as if he fills the room with energy, power and so much danger I can taste it from here. He must be six feet tall, with black, sleek hair and the darkest eyes I have ever seen. He's clean shaven and his aftershave wafts toward me like a potion designed to trap a woman's soul.

He is staring at me with an expression I can't quite read, and I feel like a moth caught in a flame because something about this man burns me up inside. What is this feeling; I've never felt it before?

Just for a moment, we stand, neither one of us saying a word as we adjust to the situation. Then he takes me by surprise and moves across to my bed and pats the space beside him.

"Sit."

He nods and from the tone of his voice, he expects me to obey and yet the way he said it was different to how I imagined. It was almost—kind.

So, I do as he says because from the look in his eyes, he has something to say that I am intrigued to hear.

I sit on the edge of the bed as far away from him as possible and stare at my hands like a naughty child. I can't look at him because this situation is the strangest I've ever been in.

Then he speaks. "You're angry, why?"

For a moment I don't answer him because now he's said it, I feel a little foolish. This man isn't used to childish games, and in that one sentence has reduced my demands to those of a petulant child.

I say in a low voice. "Is it too much to ask that you come

to my door like a gentleman and call for me properly? I'm not a delivery. I'm a person with feelings and deserve a little respect."

He is silent, and I wait with a morbid curiosity to see what he says.

Then he says wearily, "Anastasia, we have a business deal. You know that. This is not a relationship like any normal one. We are not lovers, we are strangers. The fact I'm here at all is all the respect you need. We both know what this is and I'm curious to know why you think otherwise?"

The anger starts building as I measure my response. What an asshole.

Standing, I move across to the window and once again look down on the circus that's arrived outside my door. The sadness overcomes me as I see what this is. He's right, of course. It is a business arrangement, after all and I knew that.

"Ok."

"Ok what?"

I can sense the irritation in the room and sigh.

"Ok, I'll come. You're right, Mr. Moretti, this is a business arrangement. I have something you want and you are my way out of this god forsaken place but I do have a few conditions first."

I turn around and stare at him with a bravery I don't feel inside as I see the storm in his eyes. "Name them."

"I want my freedom."

"No."

"What do you mean, no?"

"A simple word, Anastasia, that I know you understand the meaning of. You ask for freedom, but that will never happen. Let me explain. My world is a dangerous place to be. In agreeing to live in it, you leave any hope of freedom at the door. I have many enemies and you will be an attractive target for them. You have the freedom of my home, but outside you will never be alone. I have assigned a guard to protect you when you leave my walls and so, any freedom you enjoy now will be left inside this room. Any more demands—Anastasia?"

I just stare at him in disbelief as he taps his foot, indicting his impatience to get this over with. It just angers me more and I snap, "I want my own room."

"Agreed."

"I want my own car."

"Agreed."

"I want to start my own business."

"This is not Christmas, Anastasia and I'm not Santa. These demands are nothing short of stalling for time, so let me lay it on the line. I have no interest in what you do with your time when I don't demand it. You will have an allowance outside of your own income from Johnson's plastics that you can give away for all I care. The only thing I want from you is to be my wife in public. That is your job, Anastasia. Be the perfect wife in company and in private you can do what the hell you like. However, let me warn you that does not include other men. Do I make myself clear?"

"What?"

I stare at him in total disbelief as he stands and heads toward me, and from the look in his eyes, he is serious. Standing just centimeters away from me, I can feel his breath fan my face as he says in a whisper, "I have a reputation to protect and if word got out that my wife was screwing around behind my back, I would be extremely angry, darling. So, take this as a warning, you have your freedom but for one thing. You are mine, even if I don't take advantage of that. I chose you for a reason, Anastasia. I have watched you with interest over the years as you played the loyal fiancée to Sebastian Stone. We both know it was exactly the relationship I am asking of you now. In public, the happy couple and strangers in private. You have trained well for this and that is what I want most from you."

He lifts my face to his, and his touch is like electricity shooting through my entire body. It shocks it into life, and every nerve I possess is standing on edge. His lips hover over mine as he whispers, "I have watched you for a long time, and I like what I see. You are perfect for me and I know you will be the wife I deserve. Don't let me down and I will give you everything but that one thing. Love. Can you live without love in exchange for everything else, Anastasia, because I know I can?"

It's too much, too intense, and I take a step back to get some air between us. Can I live without love?

He doesn't move, and something grows between us as he invades my mind and personal space. There is nothing in this room but him and with a slight edge to my voice, I say huskily, "I have lived without love my entire life, Mr. Moretti. How can I miss what I never had in the first place?"

I dare to look up, and the storm in his eyes causes my breath to hitch as I sense something shift between us. Then he steps away and says in his sexy, deep voice, "Come, I'll send someone for your cases. Say goodbye to your old life, you will not be returning."

I follow him from my childhood room and don't look back.

I pass the framed photos in the hallway as we walk past them down the stairs.

I pass Martha looking so desperate and as if she's about to cry and I stop, pulling her to me and clinging onto the one person I will miss. Fighting back the tears, I say in a small voice, "I love you, Martha. I'll be in touch."

Just for a second, she clings to me and I feel my heart breaking. She has always been in my life, and this is the hardest thing I have to do.

She whispers, "I love you, darling. I'm always here for you, don't be a stranger."

Nodding, I don't trust myself to speak and my mom says in a fake sincere voice, "Come darling, we need to leave."

With a heavy heart, I follow them outside, my long ivory gown trailing behind me. The diamonds sparkle as the sun catches them as I step into the light. My satin shoes crunch on the gravel, as I walk behind the man who will be my husband in a few hours from now and I walk away from my home to an uncertain future and the wedding that's been arranged at a nearby church in just thirty minutes time.

Yes, today is Anastasia Johnson's wedding day and yet I am no ordinary bride. I am a sacrificial lamb to the slaughter and so, I leave any humanity I possess firmly behind me as the door to the third car is held open for me and I'm helped inside. My mom takes the seat beside me and the door slams, sealing my fate.

Tobias Moretti climbs into the car in front, and I watch my cases loaded into the first car. I don't look at Martha as we ease out of the driveway. In fact, I don't look back. I can't because it would break my heart.

CHAPTER 3

TOBIAS

Sophia looks up. "What happened?"

"It doesn't matter, she's here now."

Sophia sighs and says irritably, "You're a fool, Tobias."

"Enough!"

"No, you don't get to tell me shit. I'm the only person left who tells you how it is, and this marriage is dangerous for both of you. Call it off now and let the poor girl go. I can't believe you're doing this."

"I said ENOUGH!" I raise my voice, and she falls silent and I settle back in the seat and stare out of the window. Maybe traveling with my sister was a bad move. She always calls me out on things she disapproves of and this is the biggest one to date—my marriage.

I close my eyes and lean back and think about her—Anastasia Johnson, the woman I've chosen to marry. There is something about her that's called to me for a long time now. They all think this marriage is from a chance meeting with her mother—they are wrong. Long before her father died, I was watching Anastasia Johnson.

Back then she was playing the perfect fiancée for Sebastian Stone, her sister's boyfriend from childhood.

He never wanted her because it was always Angelica. They played a convincing role in public but never met in private. I was impressed. She was everything I was looking for. Beautiful, loyal, with impeccable manners and breeding. The fact she comes with a share of a billion-dollar company sweetens the deal, but that was just the icing on the cake. It was always her I wanted; they just don't need to know that.

"They wouldn't want this."

"I said enough, Sophia, don't make me stop this car and make you ride up front."

She laughs bitterly. "I'd like to see you try."

"Don't test me because you are seriously getting on my nerves right now. Is it too much to ask for five minutes' peace before my fucking wedding?"

She huffs and looks out of the window, and I sigh inside. Sisters think they know it all and in this case she may be right. They wouldn't want me to do this, but *they* aren't here to stop me.

I push all thoughts of my parents away because I can't deal with them now. Not today. Not after what I just saw; what I felt when I saw my bride for the first time.

When Matteo told me she asked for me, I was mildly curious. I watched her through the window and even from a distance, she was beautiful. Time didn't matter as she kept me waiting because I was mesmerized. As soon as I saw her in the flesh, she dazzled me. Standing before the window with the sunlight behind her, she looked like a goddess. Her long, silk ivory gown hugged a body that would be the ruin of any man. Her golden hair piled on top of her head, secured in place with a diamond tiara, made her look like my Queen in waiting. The diamonds that sparkled from her throat highlighted a skin of the purest porcelain and those flashing blue eyes that held so much anger in them awoke the beast in me. Yes, Anastasia Johnson is mine and never knew it and if Sophia thinks I'm giving her up, then she's badly mistaken.

Sophia sighs heavily, and I tune her out. My sister only has my best interests at heart, and I know she thinks I'm making a big mistake. She'll learn I never make mistakes, just calculated risks that usually pay off.

As expected, we reach the church five minutes before the service is due to start. The crowd that has gathered is not unexpected. I've made it no secret that I'm to be married, but only invited guests are allowed inside.

The photographers from the press are here in force, and I expect our picture will be on every news channel within the hour. Yes, this city's most eligible bachelor is about to go out of business, which was my plan all along. Marry Anastasia and take the heat off me at the same time.

I've grown tired of fending off the advances of the desperate women who throw themselves at me every day. I'm tired of pretending to be interested in their banal chatter, and I'm tired of turning up to events with another faceless woman. I want there to be just one. Her.

Yes, I'm feeling rather pleased with myself right now, and as the car draws to the curb, I congratulate myself on a well-executed plan.

Security is tight—it has to be, and I note the shaded figures of my own men keeping watch over the crowd. They will have swept the church and the surrounding area and left nothing to chance. Every guest inside will have been searched and their phones confiscated for the duration of the service. When I marry Anastasia Johnson, there will be no distractions.

Sophia sighs, "Have it your way, let the farce commence."

Matteo holds open the door and I exit into a sea of suited

guards. I take my sister's hand and help her from the car and we walk together up the red-carpeted steps to the church of Saint Andrew. Flowers decorate the entire approach and I am pleased to see my favorite red roses and white lilies are in abundance.

The priest greets us at the top of the steps and if he's nervous, he's doing a good job hiding it as he beams and offers me his hand in congratulation. "Mr. Moretti, we are honored to host your wedding."

I nod and sweep past him with no words spoken. I want to get this over with because as soon as my ring is on Anastasia's finger, she belongs to me and I'm not prepared to wait a moment more to own such a beauty.

The music starts as soon as we step foot inside the church and I note the crowded congregation looking at us approach with a mixture of awe, reverence and fear. Business associates, social contacts and people who are of some use to me but no family. There's not an empty seat in sight, and I wonder what these people make of this.

Making no eye contact, I stride to the front, followed closely by Sophia and Matteo.

Then I take my seat alongside them in the front row and wait for her to arrive.

CHAPTER 4

ANASTASIA

*T*here are crowds of people everywhere I look. Mom gasps as she sees the press and says with excitement, "This is it, darling. You've made it. I knew this marriage was the best idea ever."

I say nothing because I don't have words. The fact I'm shaking with fear next to her has obviously escaped her attention. The fact I've not said two words since we left is obviously of no consequence and the terror in my heart is apparently disguised because she is behaving like any excited mother of the bride and I couldn't hate her any more than I do now.

The noise overwhelms me as the door is opened and one of Tobias's guards offers me his hand. Immediately, a tight circle is formed around me as I step into the sunlight, and I am shielded from anyone who wishes for one glimpse of the bride.

I am ushered up the red-carpeted steps of the amazing church and can only glimpse the stunning flowers that line my journey toward my fate.

All around me people are screaming my name and helicopters buzz overhead. It's almost as if I'm a celebrity and it's a lot to deal with.

By the time we reach the entrance to the church, my heart is threatening to give out on me because all of this—it's overpowering.

Then I see a familiar face looking anxious and concerned, and my heart twists into a painful knot. "Angel."

I whisper her name and the tears burn behind my eyes as I see my sister standing waiting, clutching an enormous bouquet and looking like the angel she is named after.

The door closes behind me and mom says loudly, "Well, that was something else."

She starts fussing with my dress and saying with concern, "Look at the state of you, I hope they never got a picture of the creases in this train."

Angel steps forward and looks at me with concern. "Are you ok, honey?"

Am I ok? An innocent question, and if I give the right answer, I know she will whisk me away and hide me forever, so I lie. "I'm fine."

Grabbing my arm, she steers me to the side and whispers, "You know you don't have to go through with this. Sebastian and I have contacts and can get you away from here before they even discover you've gone. Just say the word and I'll make the call."

I smile shakily. "I said I'm fine, but thanks, it means a lot."

Angel's eyes fill with tears and she whispers, "Please don't do this, Anastasia. I'm begging you; you need to fall in love and marry a man that will make you happy. Not him. Not that criminal."

I shrug and try to muster a bravery I certainly don't feel and smile as reassuringly as I can under the circumstances. "It's fine, I want this, really I do."

She nods in defeat and hands me the exquisite bouquet

that I'm seeing for the first time. I've had no input in this wedding at all. Tobias Moretti organized everything, and my only task was to show up on the day. The dress was delivered from the finest designer and the jewels arrived a little over an hour ago. My hair and make-up were professionally done by women he arranged to come to my house and even my underwear was delivered in a tissue filled box, tied with a satin bow. He has left nothing to chance and I should be grateful, shouldn't I?

Mom stands beside me and beams proudly, and it sickens me. She is loving this—the attention and the fact it's the celebrity wedding of the year. I wish Martha were here instead of her, but mom said she had to stay home. I hate her for that.

Turning to Angel, I whisper, "I wish Martha was here."

She squeezes my hand and nods. "I know. She would want to see her little girl on her wedding day, but mom overruled us as always."

The music starts, canceling out any further conversation, and my stomach flutters as I sense my time is up. This is it, there's no going back now because the men that stand guarding the exit will make sure I see this through. There is no escape, and now I'll just have to suck it up and live with my decision.

I'm already regretting it.

Mom walks by my side and Angel follows behind. As sisters we are alike to look at, but our personalities are poles apart. She was always the adventurous one. The fearless one of the family and way smarter than me. She now runs Johnson's Plastics because my father wanted it that way. In fact, anyone but me. He was disappointed in me and that hurts the most. I was never given a chance.

As the music plays and we walk down the aisle, I am grateful for the veil covering my face. I can't look at anyone.

They aren't here for me, anyway. They are here for *him*; we are all here - for him.

Then I see the man himself, standing and watching me approach. Something happens inside me that makes my breath hitch as I see the intense look drawing me to his side. As future husbands go, many would say I hit the jackpot. Who wouldn't want this man? He has it all. Good looks, more money than we can ever spend, and social standing and acceptance in a world that should run the other way. He is dark and menacing and is watching me with a promise in his eyes. I shiver inside. A business arrangement, he said—those eyes say otherwise.

As we reach him, mom nods and I turn and hand Angel my flowers. I see the pain in her eyes and try to hold it together as she takes her place beside the man who always loved her unconditionally. I almost weep as I see the look they share and watch as his hand clasp hers tightly. Why didn't he want me when she left all those years ago? I thought he would fall in love with me with that same intensity. It's why I agreed to act as his fiancée for five long years. But he always wanted her, and when she returned, I was surplus to requirements.

Then I take my place beside the only man who has ever wanted me, and that's just my luck. He doesn't really want *me;* he wants the trophy wife I portrayed for the last five years. Now he wants the same, and I am doomed to an emotionless future with a stranger.

As the priest begins the ceremony, I don't even hear the words and just go through the motions of a service that will chain me to the man beside me. The hymns are sung and I'm sure I mouth the words but don't register what they are.

When I speak, it's soft and as expected, like any bride who can't wait to marry her one true love, but it's all an act. Then, as he slips the biggest diamond I have ever seen on my finger,

I feel the weight of it pinning me down and preventing my escape. Then I hear the words that turn the lock on my cell. "I now pronounce you husband and wife. You may now kiss the bride."

It's only then I snap out of it and turn to face the man who now controls me. He steps forward and raises the veil, and the eyes that stare at me contain a storm that threatens to destroy me. His arm encircles my waist and pulls me close, and his other hand reaches around the back of my head and locks me in position as his mouth descends to mine.

The first touch of his lips is soft and gentle, and I can smell his not unpleasant aftershave. Then he forces my lips apart and as his tongue enters my mouth, he takes mine and twists it with his, kissing me deeply, passionately and with an ownership that brands me his forever. He pulls me hard against his body, and there is no room to breathe.

I'm drowning.

He possesses me before the whole congregation, and I have no choice but to comply. There is silence all around us as he kisses me long and hard. No quick peck for him, this is full on and surely should have finished by now. I feel the heat tearing through my body as he carries on as if he is in need of this to survive.

I feel breathless, giddy and possessed and have never kissed a man like this before in my life.

Then he pulls away and his arm remains around my waist, giving me the support I need right now because my legs are trembling so much. He fixes me to his side with an iron grip as he starts the slow walk to the back of the church. He doesn't make eye contact with any of the congregation, and I feel the flush creeping over my entire body. This is so intense. *He* is intense and I almost can't breathe as I am propelled to the door and then swallowed up in a sea of black suits.

They crowd around us and let no one in. We move as a pack through the open doorway and we move at a pace. I am almost carried down the stairs into the waiting car with none of the photo opportunities couples usually enjoy.

Then the door is slammed, and the car is on the move almost as quickly as he fastens the seatbelt around me.

He turns and his eyes glitter dangerously.

"You're mine now."

CHAPTER 5

TOBIAS

Mine, how good that sounds. As I settle back in my seat, I congratulate myself on a plan that has come together better than expected. Seeing Anastasia walk toward me like a goddess was all the reassurance I needed. I knew it would be her. When I saw her for the first time, I knew it would be her. Now she's my wife I can breathe a sigh of relief because once again, I have got exactly what I want—her.

She is quiet, and I can tell she's in shock. I feel her nerves fill the car, it's all around us. I'm used to that. People are nervous of me, and rightly so.

Leaning forward, I reach for the bottle of champagne that sits neatly stowed in the compartment opposite and fill a champagne flute and hand it to my quivering bride. She takes it silently, and then I fill another and raise my glass to hers. "To us."

She looks at me with an acceptance that annoys me a little and whispers, "To us."

Then she knocks the liquid back in one move and leans back in her seat and closes her eyes.

I take a moment to stare at her gorgeous face without her knowing. Those lips that I couldn't wait a minute more to taste, tempt me once again. They are full and soft and tasted so good and I fight back the urge to have my fill again. I know I took too long when I kissed her in church. I couldn't help myself; it was all I thought of through the whole ceremony. There is something so incredibly edible about Anastasia Johnson, and for some reason I am rethinking the terms of our contract already.

Reaching out, I make to touch those lips, desperate to feel them once again, but then my hand drops. We made a deal; I can't scare her off and must practice patience.

Suddenly, her eyes snap open and I find myself staring into two pools of crystal colored water and she says in a stronger voice, "Is there any more of that?"

She holds out her glass and I fill it with a wry, "What's this, darling, are you searching for a little courage inside the bottle?"

"Do I need some?"

I say nothing because she won't like the answer I give. Yes, she will need courage and lots of it because I have a particular future mapped out for my delectable new wife and it's completely different to the one she thinks is coming.

Leaning back, I take a swig of the finest champagne and say abruptly, "I would like to remind you of the terms of our contract. You will act as my loving wife in public and that begins now at the reception. You will go through the motions of being the perfect blushing bride and then, when it ends, I will allow you to settle into your new home."

She says nothing, just nods and stares blankly ahead, and I wish I knew what was running through her mind.

Leaning back, I reach for my phone and scroll through the various messages, leaving most of them unanswered. Many are from business associates congratulating me on my wedding; I will not reply. I very rarely do. I have Sergio to do that for me. Sergio Bellini is my assistant and does most of my work for me. He is the acceptable face of my business and my front man, so to speak. He takes all the crap and keeps it from my door, and I rely on him to keep me sane in a word where sanity is just a word in a dictionary that applies to other people. My world is insane and I'm tired of it.

It's why I'm changing it slowly by buying up legitimate companies and turning things around. I'm tired of the filth I deal with on a daily basis and I'm tired of the backstabbing, plotting, and destruction that follows my shadier business practices.

"What happens next?"

Her voice is soft and yet with a strength to it that makes me smile.

"I told you, we attend our wedding reception. Then they will leave and we get on with our lives."

"Will I be free to see my family?"

"Of course, you're not in prison, Anastasia."

She nods and bites her bottom lip, and I feel my cock twitch. In fact, my cock hasn't stopped twitching since I saw her standing before me in that fucking dress. I wanted nothing more than to bend her over and sink my twitching cock inside her as she panted my name.

Shaking my head, I try to distract myself from this weird schoolboy crush I seem to have developed on this intriguing lady.

"You said I had my own room. Where will it be?"

She won't give up and I sigh. "Enough with this conversation, it's irrelevant. As soon as we deal with our guests, you can settle in."

I cut the conversation because I no longer want to make her a promise I know I can't keep because I've decided that there is no way in hell she is sleeping anywhere but with me

—she will just have to deal with that because I'm a man who always gets what he wants and she will be mine before the night is out.

Once again, my cock twitches as it senses an evening of pure, unadulterated pleasure and I smile to myself. I have a wife now and I intend on using her in every sense of the word.

Luckily, we reach our destination and the car sweeps through the gates of my fortress, where we have invited a few select guests back to celebrate with us. Mainly important business associates and Anastasia's family and a marquee has been set up in the garden to keep them out of the house. The house itself is on lockdown until the last one of them leaves because nobody sees inside my home except those that live there.

We move as always in convoy and in the car ahead of us is Sophia, who had the misfortune to travel with Mrs. Johnson. The sooner I send that vile creature packing, the better because I saw the way she treated Anastasia, and it stirred the anger within me. Even from the distance, I saw her pull her away from the window and the beast inside me growled. That's the last time anyone touches my wife but me. I will not tolerate it, and anyone who lays their hand on this woman beside me in the future will suffer the darkest consequences.

The car following us holds her sister and Sebastian Stone, the asshole who called Anastasia his fiancée for five years before me. He never wanted her, just Angelica, and it was Anastasia's father, Harvey Johnson, who engineered the whole fake relationship thing to split them up. His business partner was Sebastian's father and needed urgent lifesaving medical treatment. The bastard told him that he would pay on one condition. His son would marry the wrong daughter. It amuses me to think of the lengths he took to destroy his daughters. He wanted Angelica to harden up and take control of his business, and that didn't include Sebastian Stone. It backfired big time because Angelica ran away and returned five years later when he was dead, taking her rightful place at the head of the company I own shares in. Now that company is worth billions and Angelica and Sebastian run it together and I reap the rewards in dividends. If she wants to sell, it can only be to family, which is why I'm sitting here. I'm family now, and if anyone is taking over a billion-dollar company, it's me.

However, they all think that was the reason I married Anastasia; it wasn't. To be honest, I have other companies, I don't need this one. Mirabelle Johnson saw this arrangement as a safety net should her eldest daughter try to sell up and leave them with nothing. She thinks she controls Anastasia; she doesn't - I do.

As the car comes to an abrupt stop, I turn to my wife and say sarcastically, "Honey, we're home."

CHAPTER 6

ANASTASIA

From the moment Tobias Moretti kissed me, I have been battling something deep inside that was sparked into life as soon as his lips touched mine. I'm not sure what it is, but it's thrown me completely—I liked it.

Now, in a confined space beside the man I just committed my life to, it all feels a little surreal, and I'm struggling to make sense of it all. I was grateful for his strong arm holding me up because any strength I had deserted me the moment his lips touched mine.

When he offered me the champagne, I couldn't drink it fast enough and I could tell it surprised him.

In fact, the whole car journey was pure torture because I was so close to him. I almost couldn't breathe because he was everywhere and every one of my senses was on high alert - to him.

When I opened my eyes and saw him staring at me, I wanted to snap them shut again because what I saw in those eyes spelled danger in every way.

The moment we passed through the huge gates of my new home, I felt as if the prison door slammed shut behind me. I almost couldn't appreciate the impeccable grounds of a home that has everything a person could wish for. Beautiful landscaped gardens flashed past and the driveway alone took us ten minutes to navigate. It's like entering a small kingdom - his kingdom and I can't breathe as what I've agreed to suffocates me. All I can think of is running to my new room and locking this world out. I need to be alone to organize my crazy thoughts because Tobias Moretti is suddenly much more than just my husband, he's the enemy.

I swallow hard and my heart beats faster as the car stops in a massive courtyard.

The door opens, and he takes my hand and as I fight the urge to snatch it away, he says in a deep, controlling voice, "Come, we will greet our guests."

As I step into the light, I gasp at the mansion that stands before me. Made of the whitest stone, it stands proudly in the sunshine, glittering like the finest jewel in an impressive setting. I have never seen such a property in my life, and my heart settles a little. I could lose myself in here; I may never have to see him except in company. Maybe this won't be so bad, after all.

Once again, he pulls me close to his side but here we don't have the same close protection that followed us at the church, which settles my heart—a little.

Tobias walks at quite a pace and I struggle to keep up in the impossibly high heels he chose for me. We head through a side gate that sits beside the huge property and down some steps toward a grassed area where I see the largest marquee I've ever seen waiting for us, nestling in the impressive landscaped gardens of what can only be described as a palace.

Tobias's men follow us, and I wonder if this will always be the case. Suddenly, I stumble and feel a sharp pain as my ankle twists and I gasp. Tobias stops and looks down with concern. "What?"

"My ankle; I think I twisted it."

He looks concerned and pulls me over to a nearby bench and then kneels before me. Then I feel his hand lift the silk folds that surround me and he takes my ankle carefully and lays it across his knee. My eyes water as he gently probes the skin and says irritably, "It's just a sprain, nothing broken."

Looking over his shoulder, he snaps, "Arrange an ice pack and bring it to the marquee."

One of his men turns and speaks into a headset he's wearing and Tobias says abruptly, "Here, let me help you."

Before I know what's happening, he sweeps me in his arms and stands, holding me like a baby. I feel a little panicked because being so close to him is somewhat unnerving and I squeak, "Its fine, I'm sure I can walk."

"Nonsense." He grins wickedly. "I will take great pleasure in delivering you personally."

It feels a little awkward as I nestle in his arms, but strangely, I'm enjoying the experience. He tightens his grip and I sink further into his chest, and I can smell the scent of a man mingled with that intoxicating aftershave. I squirm inside because I feel a sudden heat traveling through my body that I'm not used to. It's as if my body has come alive and it responds by edging nearer to his and I can't stop it— it's as if it has a will of its own and he laughs softly. "Stop struggling, little bird, just enjoy the ride."

His voice is husky, and he whispers the words seductively into my ear so nobody else hears. Just being so close to him is unnerving, and I feel my heart flutter inside like a trapped bird wanting to fly.

I swear he slows down because it feels ages before we reach the opening to the marquee, and as he sweeps inside, I gasp in delight at the fairy tale before me.

He whispers, "Do you like it? I wanted it fit for a queen— my queen."

I just stare in wonder at the magical setting he has created. It's like a fairy tale palace, with chandeliers sparkling from the silken fabric that hangs from the ceiling. Beautiful flower arrangements are simply everywhere, made up of the deepest red roses and the whitest lilies. The scent is almost overpowering and the lighting soft and seductive. I see several large tables filling the space, draped in starched white tablecloths on which stand crystal glasses and impressive place settings. Silver cutlery sparkles beside the finest china and burning candles nestle inside impressive arrangements and I say with delight, "I love it."

I look around me in wonder, and he laughs softly. "Then I am happy." He sets me down gently and I gingerly test my ankle by standing on it and wince with the pain. Looking concerned, he snaps, "Where's that fucking ice pack and bring two Tylenol?"

A man scurries off and I say in surprise, "Are you always so rude?"

He just nods. "Yes."

His arm once again encircles my waist, and he holds me to his side as we stand at the entrance to fairydom and I find that all the pressure has been taken off my ankle as he holds me up. Then I see the guests trailing down the steps toward us and Tobias says huskily, "Just play your part and then you can sit and rest that ankle."

The first person to reach us is an incredibly beautiful woman. She looks amazing with her long dark hair that gleams in the sunlight and swings around her shoulders. She is wearing a deep red silk dress that clings to a shapely body and the jewels that sparkle at her throat look expensive. I watch as she kisses Tobias and whispers something in his ear, and he looks irritated. Then she looks at me and I am struck by how beautiful her eyes are. They are the deepest green and flash with an energy that takes my breath away.

Tobias says gently, "This is my sister, Sophia."

I stare at her with interest because now he has made the connection. I can see it's obvious. They share devastating good looks and a manner that tell people not to mess with them. I feel a little nervous, and she leans in and kisses me on both cheeks and whispers, "Welcome to the family, Anastasia. Remember, my door is always open."

She moves inside and I stare after her in surprise but then feel my nerves stand to attention as I hear, "Darling, you make such a lovely couple."

I sense Tobias's irritation and feel the same because mom is standing there looking like the cat who got the cream. He nods politely, and she turns to me and gushes, "My beautiful baby, your father would be so proud."

I stare in disbelief as she wipes an imaginary tear from her eye and then I hear, "Move along mother, you're holding up the line."

I almost crumble as I see my sister standing behind her and if there's anyone I want to see right now, it's her. She nods to Tobias and then moves along to me and takes me in her arms, whispering, "Are you ok, honey?"

For a moment, I cling to her and wish for nothing more than to be back in the room we shared as children with nothing but hope before us. I almost can't speak and she whispers, "Ana, honey, do you want to go somewhere and talk?"

Pulling myself together, I shake my head and try to smile with a bravery I'm certainly not feeling. "No, it's fine. Please grab a glass of champagne, we'll talk soon."

She moves away looking worried, and then Sebastian stands before me looking at me with concern. I feel Tobias stiffen beside me as he leans in and kisses me on both cheeks, murmuring, "You look beautiful, are you ok?"

I see the concern in his eyes and bite my bottom lip to

keep it from trembling as Tobias snaps, "Of course she's ok, it's her wedding day."

Sebastian stares at him with undisguised animosity and I hold my breath as Tobias snaps, "Enough, my wife needs to sit, it's been a long day."

Pulling me to his side, he sweeps through the marquee toward the top table and a waiter pulls out my chair, which I'm grateful to sit down on. Leaning in, Tobias whispers, "There are two tablets next to that glass of water. Take them for the pain and no more alcohol. They don't mix well and I need you to stay fit and well. Use the ice pack, it will take the swelling down."

He offers me the glass and as I take the tablets for the pain, Angel sits on the other side of me and snaps, "What happened?"

"I sprained my ankle; it hurts a little."

She stares at Tobias with anger, and I shake my head. "It's my fault, I never could walk in heels."

Tobias takes his seat beside me and mom sits on the other side of him which I can tell irritates him and I whisper to Angel. "I'm guessing this meal won't last long if he's got to talk to mom."

We giggle, and I start to feel a little better. Maybe it's the pills, or maybe it's the relief the worst is over, but I'm guessing it's because I have my sister by my side. Yes, we may have fallen out over the man on the other side of her, but that's in the past now. It's the future that counts now, and I have a feeling I'm going to need my sister a lot in mine.

CHAPTER 7

TOBIAS

I can't wait for this circus to be over. There is only one thing I want, and she is sitting to the right of me, deep in conversation with her sister. I have the misfortune to be seated next to her mother, and she is irritating me more than I can bear. I'm not sure why I thought this was a good idea. Maybe to show the world I have really settled down and am officially off the market. Maybe it was for appearance's sake, and maybe it was to please the woman who I now call my wife. It certainly wasn't to please me and after another conversation regarding the infernal woman's roses, I push back my chair and say, "Excuse me."

Anastasia looks up and I lean down and whisper, "Duty calls, I won't be long."

She looks surprised and whispers, "On our wedding day?"

Her eyes are wide and her bottom lip is tempting me way too much, so I give into my urge and kiss her lips softly, relishing the taste of innocence and the sweetest soul. She looks at me in shock as I stroke her cheek and stare deep into her eyes. "I won't be long."

Then I head off to get some air because I can't stand

another minute of Mrs. Johnson's company. In fact, I'm of a mind to put a contract on out her today, but I know that will never happen. She's family now, god help me and like it or not, she's here to stay.

Matteo follows me looking concerned and once we're out of earshot, I snap, "That fucking infernal woman is seriously pissing me off. What do you suggest?"

Matteo's lips twitch, and as I glare at him, he holds his hands up. "What?"

"Are you laughing at me?"

My eyes darken ominously and he stops smirking—fast. "No, Mr. Moretti."

Leaning against the wall, I remove a cigarette from my inside pocket and light it, hating myself for my weakness.

Matteo waits while I calm down and I snap, "Any news on Carlos?"

Matteo shakes his head. "Unfortunately, no."

"What about the Viper room, have they paid up yet?"

He nods, and I exhale sharply. "Is there nothing that requires my urgent attention?"

"Nothing I can think of but we can always *make* something require your attention."

Tossing the cigarette butt to the ground, I stamp on it angrily. "Just do me a favor and keep that woman away from me."

Turning my back on him, I head back to the wedding and curse the fact I ever thought this was a good idea. For once I wanted to do things the way normal people do, and now I'm regretting my generosity.

As I head back to my bride, my eye is drawn to her immediately I enter the marquee. Even from across the room, she mesmerizes me. Her head is tossed back, and she's laughing at something her sister is saying. She looks so happy it makes me smile inside and then she turns her head and sees me approaching and instantly her expression changes to one of fear and uncertainty.

As I take my seat again, Mrs. Johnson leans in and giggles. "I must say, Tobias, you have outdone yourself. Between us, I was extremely reluctant to pass over the organization of my beloved daughter's wedding to a man but..." She bats her eyelashes and purrs, "You have not disappointed me."

She stares into my eyes with a suggestive look and I look at her in disbelief—seriously, are you kidding me? This woman has no shame. I catch my sister's eye and she smirks, making me snap. "Maybe you would like to tell Sophia about your garden. She loves flowers, and these arrangements were her design."

Pointedly, I turn away toward my bride and, leaning down, whisper, "Have you had enough?"

She stares at me in shock. "What do you mean?"

"This - the guests, the wedding, everything. I can stop it now if you have."

"Have you?"

I see the hurt in her eyes and instantly regret my words. Of course, she hasn't had enough. It's the day most girls dream of, isn't it? It's why I did this after all - for her, so I nod and look over my shoulder at Matteo who is standing discreetly behind me and as he leans down, I whisper, "Tell the caterers to wrap this up and we can move to the cake."

He nods and heads off and I take Anastasia's hand and relish the huge fucking diamond I put on her finger, telling the world she is mine. Raising her hand to my lips, I kiss it gallantly and say in a low voice, "We will cut the cake and then take our first dance. After that, we will leave them to it."

I don't miss the sudden fear in her eyes and hate the fact it's there at all. Then again, she should fear me because what I have planned goes against every line of our contract.

She whispers, "Won't they think we're rude?"

"Not at all. Isn't it customary for the bride and groom to leave the wedding party for their honeymoon?"

"Honeymoon!"

Her eyes are wide and she looks like a deer caught in a hunter's sight. "Yes. Honeymoon. As I said, we do this thing right because how would it look if we didn't head straight off to a luxurious destination to get to know one another?"

Settling back in my seat, I suddenly feel in a better mood. Yes, a honeymoon. Why didn't I think of it before?

It doesn't take long to finish our meal and as I scrape back my chair, I take Anastasia's hand and help her up. I see her wince in pain and hate the fact she's injured and feel partly responsible. Once again, I anchor her to my side and whisk her off to the table where the largest cake I have ever seen stands proudly, decorated with beautiful edible flowers and crystal figurines representing the bride and groom and I love the way her eyes light up. She turns to me and I see a genuine smile as she says happily, "I love this cake, it's amazing. I can't believe how realistic the flowers are."

I feel a little puzzled because it's just a god-damned cake. I would have thought she'd react to the fuck off diamond I've put on her finger, or the ones around her neck. Not a fucking cake. But I can see she genuinely loves it and I say, "The cake pleases you more than anything?"

Her eyes shine and she nods. "I love baking. I practise it often with Martha, our housekeeper. We spend hours making little objects out of icing and marzipan, and it's such a fulfilling art. I would love to know how this cake was created."

Shaking my head, I laugh to myself. Such a simple thing pleases her far more than all the riches I have showered on her so far. She surprises me yet again.

The photographer I hired for the event calls for us to cut the cake, and I take the knife and offer it to my blushing bride. Then I wrap my hands around hers and stand behind as we smile for the camera and cut the cake in one fluid movement. Then I take a small sample of the cake and feed it to her, loving the pleasure the taste brings to her face. She savors it and I find myself itching to see that look in her eyes as she sucks my cock, but then the music interrupts a pleasant daydream and I say softly, "Our first dance. Come."

I lead her by the hand to the small dance floor and pull her hard against me. She shivers a little, and I feel her tremble under my touch as the soft music begins to play. The lights are dimmed and we could be alone as I twirl her around the dance floor in my arms. I can feel her heat through the thin layer of silk and picture the lingerie I selected myself underneath. I rub her back where the fabric parts, revealing her velvet soft skin, and she shivers a little. She feels so soft and desirable under my touch, and I am impatient to move things on.

Leaning down, I nip her neck and she gasps, "What are you doing?"

"Playing my part and remember, I expect you to do the same."

She stiffens in my arms as I lower my lips to hers and once again taste the sweetness within. At first, she is like a frozen ice sculpture that slowly begins to thaw. As she relaxes in my arms, she dares to kiss me back, and I forget that we aren't alone. I kiss her hard and bite her bottom lip a little and hear a soft groan that almost makes me lose my mind. Yes, this little bird is about to discover just what she signed up for and I'm done waiting.

CHAPTER 8

ANASTASIA

I'm not sure what's happening, but I like it. Tobias Moretti has surprised me. He is nothing like I thought he'd be. I'm not sure what it is, but he appears almost human and so far today, everything he's done has made me feel like a princess. He came to my room like I asked, even though I knew it was something he would never normally do. This whole wedding that he organized is straight out of the story books and he has played the kind, loving husband perfectly until now. In fact, as I spin around the dance floor in his arms, with his lips on mine, even I could believe this marriage wasn't a sham and the happy couple were deeply in love.

The most surprising thing of all is the way my body reacts to his touch. It's as if it has a will of its own and lights up the second he touches me. I find myself leaning into him, desperate to feel his hard body against mine. The feeling of his lips on mine when he kisses me makes me feel invincible. His touch sears my skin and brings it alive and his kiss—it binds me to the man forever, much more than any ring on my finger. Could I be developing feelings for this man?

The song changes, but he doesn't let go. Instead, he carries on and once again, I am grateful for the support he gives me because my legs are fading fast. How does he do this, how does he own me so completely after just a few hours in his company? Am I that desperate to crave just a second of his time because I have never been the one who men desired? I was always second best and tried a little too hard to get what I saw other people had. I wanted the fairy tale and when I was Sebastian's fiancée; I thought it was my time. Finally, I would be the one who got the hottest guy. I would be the envy of everyone and somebody would love me, Anastasia Johnson, unconditionally. But it wasn't to be and yet here, spinning around this fairy tale wedding with any woman's wet dream, almost makes me think dreams do come true.

I can feel his interest against the thin silk fabric of the dress he chose for me, and I'm grateful for the subdued lighting because it causes me to blush. Imagine being with a man like this. Imagine being with a man at all because, unbelievably, I never have. My virginity is something I always protected, so I could surrender it to the man I love. I always thought that man was Sebastian, but he didn't want it. He didn't want *me* and so, here I am in my early twenties and still a virgin.

I wonder if my husband knows that. Would he laugh, would it disgust him? I wouldn't be surprised. Men like women who are sexy and bold. I see them everywhere, secure in the knowledge they know what to do to keep a man's interest.

Then it hits me. I may never find that secret out. My new husband made it clear this was a business arrangement, and this is all for show. The one condition was I didn't screw around behind his back.

Suddenly, the dream fades as I realize all of this is just a show. His attention, the wedding, the dancing and the kiss—all show he doesn't want me. The inexperienced daughter of a dead man. He wants the trophy wife and as I deal with the bitter tears that burn behind my eyes, my fairy tale turns into a horror story.

"What's wrong, little bird?"

His voice is slightly husky and but a whisper, and I feel my heart breaking. "I'm sorry, I feel a little unwell."

Immediately, he stops and pulls back, and I see the dark clouds form in his eyes. "Then we must go."

In mid-song, he pulls me from the dance floor and the first person we see is my mother who hovers on the sidelines and says in a sickly sweet voice, "My turn now."

"Excuse me?"

Tobias's tone is sharp, and she giggles like a teenager. "The mother of the bride always dances with the groom, it's tradition."

"Not today, we're leaving." He is abrupt and I see the surprise in mom's eyes as he pulls me past, leaving her open-mouthed, staring in confusion, as we exit the dance floor at speed.

Angel rushes over and grabs my arm. "What's going on?"

Tobias regards her coolly. "My wife is feeling unwell. She needs to rest. Just give her some space and carry on."

"Is this true, are you feeling ok, honey?"

Angel looks anxious and I feel bad and try to smile reassuringly. "It's fine. I just feel a little light-headed. I'll go for a lie down and hopefully be back soon."

Once again, Tobias pulls me away before she can comment and then his army of guards move behind us, preventing anyone else from getting near. We walk from the marquee in a protective bubble of menace, and I feel my heart thumping as I hear the whispers all around me and pass the knowing smirks on the faces of the guests that watch us go. They think we - oh my god, they think we're going to do *that*.

It must have been the way we were dancing, because it felt as if Tobias was making love to me for everyone to see. I actually think I groaned out loud at one point. What if they heard me?

I'm grateful for the wall of menace that surrounds us because I can't face these people now. What must they be thinking?

As we leave the party, the silence descends on us like an eerie promise. Now we are heading toward the house, and I feel strangely nervous as to where he's taking me. My ankle is throbbing and I wince as I stumble after him and then, once again, I am swept into his arms and he doesn't even break his stride for a second. I snuggle into his arms, feeling completely overwhelmed by everything that's happened today and feel grateful for the comfort he's giving me. I feel safe in these strong arms and as if the world is kept locked outside and nothing can harm me here.

Then we are inside and the guards melt away, revealing what can only be described as a palace.

I look around me in astonishment as I see the palatial home of a king. This place is impeccable, beautiful and so decadent, it takes my breath away. Ornate furniture and old paintings decorate a space that has to be seen to be believed. It's absolutely huge, and I blink as the full force of it hits me. We glide effortlessly along a huge polished marble floor toward a grand staircase that forks at the top. Tobias heads left and we travel along a long corridor that has several doors standing like undiscovered secrets as they guard what's inside. We reach the end and he kicks open one of the doors, revealing another staircase and once again carries me effortlessly up another staircase into a large reception room at the top.

Huge silk drapes cover what must be a window, and regency furniture sits proudly around the room that is decorated in the palest blue. He doesn't stop there. Still holding me like the most precious piece of porcelain, he kicks open another door and I swallow hard because there is no mistaking this room.

The biggest bed I've seen in my life dominates the room, dressed in white silken sheets with a crystal encrusted coverlet, dressing the simplicity of the silk in riches. The carpet is of the brightest white and the drapes at the window are heavy silk, weighted down so they hang in folds of luxury. Either side of the bed are two tables holding the largest lamps I have ever seen bathing the room in serenity and the smell, it takes me a moment to place it and then it hits me—this room smells like him. I look up at him in surprise as he carefully lowers me onto the bed and stands back, his eyes flashing with a wickedness I would be a fool to ignore. Then he says in that sexy, husky voice that does things to me I never thought possible, "Alone at last."

CHAPTER 9

TOBIAS

Things are working out rather well. For me, anyway. Unwittingly Anastasia has given me everything I wanted, because the moment she said she was feeling unwell was my escape from a nightmare.

I didn't hesitate for a second and swept through that marquee like a tornado, leaving no room for conversation because I had only one destination in mind. My bedroom.

Now I have her exactly where I want her and feel like the king I am, in this house, anyway. She sits looking up at me with that damned trembling lip and eyes wide with fear, and the feral beast inside me roars. I have never wanted anyone as much as I do Anastasia Johnson, which surprises me. When I started this whole charade, it was to tick a box. Provide a wife to keep the wannabees away and continue to go about my daily business. I had no intention of actually spending any time with her and certainly not in this room, but here we are. I've surprised myself because I never saw this one coming.

The bed sags as I sit beside her and take her small hand in mine. She says almost fearfully, "Where am I?"

"Your new home."

"Yes, but *where* exactly; is this my room?"

I nod and her eyes dart around her nervously and the devil in me enjoys her fear. I can taste it, and it's traveling straight to my throbbing cock. I want her so badly it's becoming impossible not to revert to the beast I am and take her now. But I remind myself I'm not *that* man who takes an unwilling woman, and when I do, she will beg me for it.

She licks her lips nervously. "What happens now?"

She almost can't look at me, and I see her chest heaving as she begins to understand what a dangerous situation she is now in.

"You rest."

"And you?"

Reaching out, I touch her cheek softly and love the way her pupils dilate and her breathing intensifies. "What do you want me to do, little bird?"

She looks at me with a mixture of heat and fear, and it's a powerful combination. She can't answer me because she is torn. On the one hand, she wants me to leave so she can gather her confused feelings around her like a shield. Then again, she wants me to stay so badly she doesn't even realize it herself, and that tells me I made the right decision in choosing her. She wants me and doesn't really understand the implications, which gives me the strength to see this through.

Tilting her face to mine, I lean in and inhale her fear. Her body is trembling like a frightened animal, and I fucking love it. The power I hold over this frightened creature is turning me on so much I almost give into it - almost and so, I pull back and say gently, "You will find everything you need in the closet through that door. I had your things brought over, along with some new ones. Make yourself at home, I have business to attend to."

She stares at me in shock and I am heartened to see a flash of disappointment cloud her beautiful eyes. "You're leaving. Will we return to the party? What about my family, I never said goodbye?"

She looks hurt and afraid and I feel like the biggest bastard in the world and do something completely out of character.

"I'll call for your sister. You can say goodbye here."

She nods and I see her relax a little. Yes, she can wait—*we* can wait because when I claim my beautiful bride, she will be on her knees begging me to.

I leave her sitting on my bed and head outside. The sooner they all leave, the better, but even I know I must see this night through.

Matteo falls into step beside me as soon as I reach the back door, and I laugh softly. "One bride delivered to her new prison."

He says nothing, and he's right not to pass comment. I may be respectable to the outside world but inside my home, my life and at the head of this family, they know I'm the biggest bastard that ever lived. I'm not proud of who I am and the things I've done. I've done them all, which is why they fear me so much. Now I'm tired of it all, which is why I started buying up reputable companies and creating a new world to live in. It's why I want a wife, because I'm bored with being the most eligible guy in a room. Don't get me wrong, I always have an attractive companion by my side who I fuck mercilessly as a reward for her time. Never here though. They never see inside my home, which is why the thought of that quivering beauty upstairs in my bed is turning me on so much. New territory that feels good.

The first person I see is Sophia, who pulls me aside and hisses, "What the hell's going on, where's Anastasia?"

"She's feeling unwell and is resting."

She narrows her eyes. "What are you playing at, Tobias? This isn't you, any of it. What's really going on in that fucked-up brain of yours?"

"Don't question me, Sophia; never question me. I have my reasons and I don't need to explain them to you. Now, if you'll excuse me."

I leave her fuming behind me and feel irritated. Family, like an unwanted virus, they cling to you and no amount of shaking can get them to leave. Although I love my sister, I can't stand her sometimes and this is one of those times. She makes me look at myself differently and I don't like it. She pulls me apart and makes me question my decisions, but she's all I've got since… I push the thoughts away. Not today. Not ever.

So, I distract myself as usual and head over to Angelica and note the wariness in her eyes as I say shortly, "Matteo will take you to your sister. She needs you."

Her stupid mom overhears and cries, "Oh my poor darling, I should go to her."

"No."

Angelica holds up her hand firmly. "I'll go to her and then if she needs you, I'll come and get you."

"What do you mean, *if* she needs me, of course she needs me, I'm her mother?"

Angelica throws her a withering look and hisses, "When it suits you. No, I'm going to her. Where is she?"

Matteo steps forward and says softly, "Follow me."

I watch them head off and then feel immediately irritated as Mrs. Johnson says in a stupid girly voice, "Maybe we can have that dance you owe me."

"No."

I turn around and leave her standing looking after me with a furious expression, and the first person I see is Sebastian Stone who nods coolly. "Mr. Moretti, congratulations on your wedding."

He doesn't like me; he never has and doesn't even try to disguise it, so I say in a firm voice. "We need to talk."

He nods and follows me outside, a short distance away from the party, and as the silence surrounds us, I take another cigarette from my jacket and offer one to him. "No thanks, I don't smoke."

He looks at me with the smug pity of a man who looks down on those with a weakness, and it irritates me because he's right to do so. Tossing the cigarette away, I snap the case shut and put it in my pocket. "You're a wise man, Sebastian, which is why I'm confused."

"About what?"

"My new wife. You were her fiancé for five years and yet, to my knowledge, never wanted her in the first place. How can I admire a man who's a fool?"

His eyes flash angrily and he snaps, "Because it was never my choice. You see, Mr. Moretti, it's all very well getting what you want, but it's what you do with it when you get it that counts. I never wanted Anastasia, I was made to agree to marry her and present an image to the world of the happy couple. We were never that couple, as I'm sure you will understand. You see, you are taking up where I left off and let me tell you, it won't end well. That poor woman will be destroyed even more than she is already because a person can't live without love, Mr. Moretti, no matter how much you think they can."

"Love."

I almost spit the word to the ground to join my cigarette. "What makes you think I want love. I never have and never will. You see, that's where we're different, Sebastian. You were in love and lost it. It's all you could think about. You wanted it back, and so you agreed to that farce of an engagement to bide your time. Don't lecture me on ruining a young girl's life because you've walked in my shoes."

"I had no choice."

His voice raises an octave, and I stare at him coolly. "We all have choices in life, and Anastasia has made hers. Don't worry about her life because she will never want for a better one. I called you out here to warn you."

I relish the look in his eye as he faces me with a stony expression, as his name suggests. "You will stay away from my wife now and in the future. You are her sister's boyfriend, partner, fiancé, call it what you like but you will never touch my wife again. Do I make myself clear?"

"Touch her. What the fuck are you talking about?"

"Earlier today you touched my wife and kissed her on the cheek."

"As a fucking greeting, are you mad?"

Feeling my eyes flash, I step toward him and love the way he stands his ground, facing me with a hard expression. I move within an inch of him and he doesn't flinch, which makes me respect him a little more. Then I whisper darkly, "I repeat, you never touch my wife again because you haven't earned the right. You destroyed that woman, and if you touch her once more, I will destroy you. We may be business partners, Mr. Stone and possibly brothers-in-law in the future, but we will never be friends. So, stay away from my wife because I have no loyalty and you don't want to discover what I mean by that."

Shaking his head, Sebastian laughs bitterly, "Now I know the rumors are true, you are a heartless bastard."

Straightening up, I nod. "I never pretended to be anything else. Now, I must be returning to my guests. Thank you for coming, Mr. Stone."

I leave him standing and head back inside, keen to catch up with a few more business associates. However, I only have one thought on my mind - wrapping this show up quickly so I can get back to the real reason I did all of this—my blushing bride.

CHAPTER 10

ANASTASIA

I'm still sitting on the bed when I hear, "Ana, where are you?"

"I'm in here."

My heart leaps as Angel rushes into the room, looking so concerned it brings tears to my eyes. She rushes across and sits beside me where Tobias sat before and hugs me close. "What did he do?"

I stare at her in surprise. "Nothing, why?"

She exhales with relief and says angrily, "I don't know, there's something so off about that man. I thought maybe…"

Reaching out, I grasp her hand tightly and say softly, "He's done nothing. In fact, he hasn't put a foot wrong all day. You know, if anything, he's surprised me."

"In what way?"

"I don't know. I suppose I was expecting a monster. I'm not stupid and heard the rumors about him. I've seen the press coverage and believed every word but to me…"

"Yes?"

"Well, he's proven to be the perfect gentleman."

OWNING BEAUTY

Angel looks at me in disbelief, and I laugh. "Hard to believe I know but he has."

My ankle throbs and I wince with the pain and she looks concerned. Lifting my dress, I note the huge ugly bruise that's forming and kick off my heels in disgust. "Remind me to never wear heels like this again."

I wince, and she laughs—a little.

Looking around, she whistles in appreciation. "This place is impressive."

I grin. "You could say that."

"Have you looked around yet?"

"No, I've just sat on this comfy bed and to be honest, would be happy to stay here all night. I'm exhausted."

Angel looks worried. "You will be ok, won't you?"

I'm not so sure, but plaster a fake smile on my face. "Of course, why wouldn't I be?"

She looks a little nervous and I say softly, "Listen, what happened with Sebastian is in the past. We all know it was an impossible situation and one that was out of our hands. He never loved me, and I was in love with the dream. I wanted what you had and thought when you left, I could slot into your place and he would want me like *that*. He never did—no one ever has, and this…"

I wave my hand around, "Is a compromise worth having."

"No, it's not."

"Excuse me." I see the look on her face, and she appears upset. Taking my hand, she squeezes it tightly. "Nothing compares to finding love, Ana. Not all the riches in the world can compensate for that. I want you to find your prince, not the poor substitute. How can you be happy if you never find love? You may enjoy what wealth brings for a little while, but then you will quickly tire of it. You'll become disillusioned and bitter, and that's when the rot seeps into the cracks and starts to tear you apart. Tobias Moretti is not a man capable of love—it's obvious. He may desire you physically, but I doubt he has the capacity to know what love really means. You have never found it and are settling for a poor second."

"It's too late now." I laugh bitterly. "I've made my choice and we're surrounded by it."

I lay my head on her shoulder and she wraps a protective arm around me. "Don't worry, Angel. I've trained for this all my life. I'll be ok. He's not so bad, anyway, and has promised he'll look after me if I play my part. And I will, because it's all I know. Even as kids, I tried to be the perfect daughter. I did what I was told to and never questioned it. When I was told to marry Sebastian, I did that too because I have always wanted to please. Even now I'm going with it because it's the end of a long painful road. Now I'm married I can stop looking and concentrate on doing what makes me happy instead."

"And what will make Ana happy?"

Angel rubs my shoulder and I say lightly, "Looking around this fuck off room will make me happy. Come on, let's see what he's got."

The atmosphere shifts as we revert back to the sisters we were many years ago.

Ignoring my throbbing ankle, I pull her from the bed and we start exploring the palatial room.

Through the door in the corner is the biggest bathroom I have ever seen. We both share an excited look as we take in the white marble and chrome fittings of a bathroom that looks as if it's never been used. A roll top bath stands proudly against a huge window, and Angel jumps in and stretches out with contentment. "I could live in this bath tub alone."

I giggle and run in and out of the walk-in shower and gasp. "This is amazing."

Sinking my face into a huge fluffy white towel, I revel in the warmth it provides as I snatch it from the heated rail.

OWNING BEAUTY

We open the cupboards and see every lotion and potion a girl could need and I squeal with excitement as I share a little sample with my sister and we breathe in the heavenly scent.

Racing through another door, I gasp in delight as I find myself in the biggest walk-in closet I have ever seen. Wall to wall cupboards hide more clothes than I have ever owned in my life and mine are hanging beside new dresses, sweaters, trousers and coats all in their protective wrapping. Angel squeals as she reveals a whole wall of shoes and matching handbags and pulls open glass drawers that hold delicate pieces of lingerie, soft and silken to the touch.

We explore further and pull out slimline velvet-lined boxes of glittering necklaces and bracelets, and I have never seen anything like it. Soft lighting creates a calming atmosphere, and deep white scatter rugs soothe my aching feet.

"What's through there?"

Angel points to another door in the corner and I shrug. "Open it and see."

As she does, we walk through and my heart thumps as I see a room much like the man who owns it. An identical closet to mine, but this is all man. Darker wood cabinets hide the secrets of the man I married. Impeccable Italian suits, mainly black, sit proudly on hangers and starched shirts of every color hang like soldiers with not a crease in sight.

Angel whispers, "We shouldn't be in here."

I nod and back away, almost as if I'm backing away from the man himself.

We reach the sanctuary of my room and she looks at me with concern. "Um... honey."

I know what she's about to say and wish she wouldn't voice what is now very apparent. "It appears that you are sharing this room, are you ok with that?"

My heart starts pounding and I laugh nervously. "I'm sure

you're wrong. Maybe there was another door we never saw to his own suite of rooms. He told me I'd have my own. Maybe this *was* his, and he's moved elsewhere."

Angel doesn't look convinced and I share her concern. His things were also in the bathroom and his closet is set off mine. Maybe I'm wrong, I must be because he promised I'd have my own room. Then again, the thought of sharing this space with such a man is suddenly not an unpleasant one. I shock myself by suddenly feeling quite heated at the thought of it. Am I expected to share a bed with my new husband when he promised me my own room? I'm guessing I am because I saw the look in his eye when he placed me on this bed and it makes my heart beat faster and my legs tremble. Tobias Moretti looked at me like the master of all he surveys and I am no different to anything else in this house—this room. I am one of his possessions—he owns me and I fell right into his trap and lack the experience to know what the hell to do about it.

CHAPTER 11

TOBIAS

An hour later, I instruct Matteo to wrap this up and make sure everyone leaves, because I'm not wasting a moment more of my time. I have somewhere else I'd much rather be and can't think of anything else.

As I head back to the house, Sophia follows me and sighs heavily. "Thank god that's over, what made you put us through that."

"That, my dearest sister, was my fucking wedding. Show some respect."

"Oh, is that what it was, forgive me, but don't weddings usually involve two people who love each other? Don't dress up this business arrangement as a wedding, Tobias. We all know why you really married Anastasia and it wasn't because you love her."

We reach the back of the house and I snarl, "What I do is my business. If I want to marry, I will, and there's nothing you can do about it. I have my reasons and they're mine to know."

"No, Tobias, your reasons affect every single one of us who trails after you and obeys your commands. You're wrong to do this and you know it. Why drag a poor innocent girl into this—family? You'll destroy her in seconds and you're better than that."

I take a deep breath because right now I want to kill this irritating woman, but she's all I've got, so I measure my response carefully.

Sighing, I turn to face her and say evenly, "What's your problem?"

"Excuse me?"

"Your problem. Since the moment you found out about my plans, you've been bitching about it. I thought you'd be pleased to have another woman around the place. I thought you'd be happy that I had the distraction, and I thought you'd be on my side because you're the only family I have left."

She shakes her head and I see the emotion in her eyes as she leans back against the wall and sighs. "I want you to be happy. God knows I want it more than anything but this—it's not right. You've turned into a machine and you think you can control everything, even love."

"Who said anything about love?"

She steps toward me and takes my arm. "You need love, Tobias. *I* need love. We all need it and you have made it your business to cancel any love in our lives because you can't deal with the pain it brings."

"Enough!"

I turn away because this conversation is over as far as I'm concerned. Her voice follows me inside. "Please, I'm begging you, set the poor girl free, it's not fair on either of you."

I slam the door and stride to my room, and I hope for their sakes nobody steps in my way. Love—she knows nothing. Love is the greatest weapon that can slay a man to the bone. It strips him bare and leaves him with nothing. Love destroys an otherwise strong man and renders him an idiot, and there is no room in my life for love—ever. Sophia knows

OWNING BEAUTY

this, they all know what love did, and she dares preach to me about letting it in again. I will never love again and will spend my life hardening my heart against it. I don't need it and I don't want it and it concerns me to think she does.

As I reach the stairs to my private suite of rooms, I stand for a while to calm down. Fucking sister, she's ruined my good mood with her talk of love.

Thinking of the woman waiting in my bed soothes my anger—a little. She intrigues me. So vulnerable and afraid, and yet she has a strength inside her that has carried her through life. Every knock she's taken, she stood right up again and carried on. It must have hurt being used by her parents all her life. Given to two men to play a part, with no regard for her feelings at all. That was what drew me to Anastasia Johnson in the first place, and when I discovered the woman inside her, I liked what I saw very much. Sophia's wrong. Anastasia is perfect for me in every way and where I was interested in her for only one thing before, that changed when I saw her at the window in her wedding gown. Now I want her in every sense of the word, and I'm not one to hang around.

Feeling calmer, I head toward my bedroom. Her sister left with Stone an hour ago, so I expect she is settled in by now.

As I walk into my personal space, I note the subdued lighting and the sense of calm all around. I feel impatient to see her and head to my bedroom, hoping she is still wearing the dress because I want to peel every delicious layer of silk off that body that begs me to come and get it and I want to take my time.

As I walk into the room, she is standing by the window with a glass of what looks like champagne in her hand and without turning around says, "You promised I'd have my own room."

The sight of her standing with her back to me, with the

silk fabric clinging to her curves, does something strange to me that I have never felt before. I want this woman more than anything I've ever wanted before, and I've wanted a lot. Women throw themselves at me and it's no fun anymore, but this—this is different and I like every minute of it.

"You have your own room."

I speak softly as if I'm afraid I'll scare the exotic creature who stands before me, and as she turns, the blood roars to my cock as I see the goddess standing before me. The diamonds glitter and her chest heaves and those baby blue eyes are filled with anger and disappointment. I can't stop staring at her because I have never seen the like of her before and she sets the glass down and says defiantly, "Then you're in my room."

"No, darling, this is *our* room. Your room that I promised you is next door filled with your things and a few surprises. You see, always remember when negotiating a contract to pay attention to the finer details. In this case, I have delivered what I promised because you didn't stipulate what room you desired."

Her eyes flash and for the first time I see the steel running through her veins as she hisses, "You bastard. You know full well what I meant."

"I did. I will not deny that. Maybe you will learn a valuable lesson from this."

She turns and slips on her shoes and says tightly, "Then I'll return home. Please call me a cab because I am not staying here, in this bed, with you."

She makes to pass me and I reach out and grab her arm and say firmly, "I told you little bird, you have no freedom outside of these walls. You are my wife whether you like it or not and that means sleeping in my bed."

She makes to slap me hard across the face, and I grab her arm and relish the fear enter her eyes. Then I pull her roughly toward me and whisper, "I also told you that I would not harm you. If you think I'm the sort of man to force himself on a woman, then you don't know me. Relax, my love, because sleep is the only thing I have in mind. Think for a moment, how would it look, my bride spending her wedding night back at her childhood home. We made a deal, and you signed on the dotted line. It would be all over the gutter press if we spent our wedding night apart, and that includes inside this house. So, back down and accept this is how it's going to be and for the record, my little bird, I said you would beg for it first and the only question that remains is how long that will take you?"

I release her and she stands looking so furious I just stare at her in awe. She is impressive, beautiful and everything I could ever want from a woman. Yes, this day is turning out to be better than expected because now the chase is on and I'm a hunter by nature and always get my prey.

CHAPTER 12

ANASTASIA

I go to my room. Not the one I thought I'd be spending the night in, but the one he agreed was mine. I'll show him he can't call the shots and try to twist the terms of our contract. Bastard!

If I could lock the door, I would, but there isn't one, so I drag a chair over the door and wedge the handle under it. Then I rip the diamonds from around my neck and the tiara from my hair. I am so angry I almost can't breathe as I think of ways to inflict a long, slow, painful death on the back stabbing bastard I just married.

Still muttering curses under my breath, I step out of my wedding gown and scrunch it into a ball and throw it angrily across the room. Then I rip the underwear off and grab my sweatpants and sweatshirt from the cupboard that somebody arranged so neatly. Quickly, I take my hair down and let it fall around my shoulders and then sit like a petulant child on the small couch that occupies the corner of the room.

Drawing my knees to my chest, I wrap my arms around them and allow emotion to have its moment. The tears fall freely as I find myself in a situation completely out of my control.

I feel so alone and when Angel left; it tore my heart out because that signified the end of everything I knew. Now I'm stuck in a gilded cage with a back stabbing bastard and I have no one.

I'm not sure how long I sit crying for before I realize nobody has even tried to check on me. I may as well have saved myself the trouble because he hasn't tried to get in once. Wiping my tears away, it dawns on me that maybe he does have some sense of fairness and will respect the fact I'm in my own space and leave me alone.

So, I curl up on the couch and settle down because if he thinks I'm going in there and sleeping with him, then he's got another thing coming.

∽

MY ACHING limbs wake me in the early hours, along with my throbbing ankle. The pain is intense and I realize I don't have any painkillers, or even water to drink and feel a little dehydrated. Stretching out, I wince as the pain hits me and I curse my bad luck. Great, now I'll have to sneak out of here and look for something to take the edge off my pain.

There are no windows in the walk-in closet, so I don't even know what time it is. Erring on the side of caution, I drag the chair away from the door, grateful for the soft carpet that absorbs the sound and quietly open the door. The bathroom is bathed in a ghostly light as I pass through the large space toward the bedroom door. Gingerly, I open it and see the room's in darkness. It's so dark I can't see if he's sleeping and listen out for any signs of life.

I can't hear anything and just tiptoe in the direction of the door and hope to god he doesn't wake up and see me.

I manage to negotiate the bedroom and find my way to the little room off it that is also as black as the night sky. My ankle is killing me, reminding me that the earlier pain killers are now a distant memory, and I creep toward the door to the stairs.

My heart thumps with fear as I carefully open it and hope to god, I don't miss my footing and stumble down them. My adrenalin levels are running high as I reach the bottom step and the passageway on the level below. Now I'm here, I feel a little afraid. It feels wrong to be creeping through his house in the dead of the night, but I have needs that I can't ignore.

It's difficult to find my way in a strange home, but I head downstairs, hoping to find the kitchen to get what I need.

It's so dark, but there are a few lights to aid my progress as I tiptoe stealthily through the house.

It feels like an adventure and I'm relishing it because my life has been as dull as ditch water up until this point.

As my feet touch the marble floor of the hallway, I feel euphoric. I made it.

Now I just need to find the kitchen.

As I walk through the large open space, I stare around me in wonder. This place - it's like nothing I've ever seen before. Who lives like this?

Each door opens into an impressive room that I wish I had longer to explore, but I'm on a mission that can't wait.

Finally, I reach the kitchen and then stare in disbelief as Tobias faces me from the huge breakfast bar that dominates the room and says firmly, "There are two Tylenol and a glass of water here for you. Mrs. Billings has left you a sandwich because you must be hungry and there's coffee in the pot."

My mouth falls open because it's obvious he was expecting me. Then I notice that he has changed and my mouth falls open for a different reason. He's wearing black sweat pants with a tight-fitting t-shirt. His huge biceps are resting on the counter and they are totally covered with black intricate tattoos that must have been painful to create. His hair is slightly messy on top and the stubble on his jaw is sexy as hell. He is barefoot and sits in his home like a sleeping tiger because his eyes flash with power as he directs the full force of it to me.

He points to the seat across from him and says firmly, "Sit. You must be hungry and in pain."

I say nothing and just head toward him because even I know I'd be a fool to ignore my own needs. As I slip onto the stool, he slides the water toward me and says, "Take the pills then make sure you eat."

My stomach growls, reminding me I've neglected it and the sight and smell of the sandwich is too much, and I fall on it like a ravenous beast. I don't look at him, acknowledge him, or speak because as far as I'm concerned, he has to earn it first. Then again, I feel a little foolish because from the moment we met he has been nothing short of a gentleman. He may have tricked me with the room, but aside from that, he has behaved impeccably and catered to my every need. I feel a little bad as he sits beside me staring at his laptop and remember my manners and say softly, "Thank you."

He looks up with questions in his eyes and I half smile.

"For the wedding, I never thanked you. It was beautiful."

He leans back and looks at me with those deep, dark eyes, and I feel as if I'm drowning.

Then he nods. "You're welcome."

He looks back to his computer and I take a sip of the coffee he poured for me and say. "And thank you for the lovely closet. You have been very generous."

Again, he just looks up and nods. "It was my wedding gift to you."

I stare at him in surprise, and he laughs. "Sorry it wasn't wrapped."

I say nothing and just sip the hot drink, feeling a lot calmer than I did before and just a little foolish.

He looks down again and I wonder what he's working on so late at night.

I try again. "Couldn't you sleep?"

"I was waiting for you."

"Me?"

Sighing, he snaps the laptop shut and stares at me with a twinkle in his eye that makes my breath hitch. "I knew you would come out eventually for food or some form of pain relief. I just waited here until you did."

"Am I really so predictable?"

"Yes."

He grins to take the sting from his words, and I laugh softly.

Looking around, I stare in awe at the huge, decadent kitchen that stretches the width of the entire house. It's like a great hall filled with expensive gadgets and handmade carpentry. Granite worktops gleam and the chrome and stainless-steel shine and the chandeliers that hang from the ceiling sparkle in the lamplight.

I nod toward his computer. "Do you always work into the night?"

"Mostly."

I stare at him in surprise, and he shrugs. "I can't sleep. It's a problem that I gave up trying to solve years ago. Mainly I work in my bedroom suite but knew you'd be needing this so brought it downstairs."

I feel bad and again a little ashamed and he says softly, "Don't."

"What?" I look at him in surprise and he smiles softly. "Don't feel bad because you had every right to be angry."

I'm not sure what to say because this man is surprising me with every word spoken.

"You are nothing like I imagined you to be."

He laughs. "That's good to know."

"Why is it?"

"Because I know my reputation, Anastasia, and it's not a good one. To be honest, I was intrigued to find you agreed to this wedding at all. Then I met your mother, and I understood."

He winks and I laugh a little and he says huskily, "It's good to hear you laugh."

"Is it?"

"Contrary to what you may think, little bird, I only want what's best for you. Now, at the risk of you storming back to the closet, may I suggest you get some sleep. We have a long day tomorrow and need to be up early."

"Why, what's happening?"

I feel the nerves return and his eyes flash as he stands and takes my hand, pulling me with him.

"I told you, tomorrow we go on our honeymoon. You asked me what I was working on so late into the night. It was the arrangements for our trip. Now we need to rest."

"But…"

He pulls me along with him and I fight hard to get a breath. Honeymoon? What on earth is he playing at?

However, it soon dawns on me that I have a more urgent problem to deal with first because it appears that my new husband has decided he also needs to sleep and as we approach the bedroom, I feel the anxiety grip me hard.

We head into the room and I feel the nerves return as he nods toward the bed. "Which side do you sleep on?"

I feel so embarrassed and shrug, "You choose."

I swallow hard as he pulls his shirt off and my mouth waters as I see the strong chest decorated with even more tattoos and the perfect six pack dancing before my eyes.

He winks and says cheekily, "Don't worry, I'll keep the pants on, for tonight, anyway."

I feel myself blushing as he pulls back the sheets and says with a challenge in his eyes, "In."

Swallowing hard, I decide to just suck it up and quickly jump into the bed and edge as close to the side as possible, still fully dressed.

It appears to amuse him because he laughs softly and turns out the lamp, saying with amusement, "Sleep well my darling."

Now the room is in darkness, I can start to relax. The bed is huge and he could be in the next room, given the space between us. Maybe I was overreacting. After all, he's right. How would it look? It didn't mean he was going to pounce on me. I feel the heat tearing through me as I think about what that would mean. He wouldn't be so happy then when he discovers his new bride is totally clueless about how to please a man. I'm guessing he wouldn't feel lucky and the tears burn behind my eyes as I feel such a failure. I must be the oldest virgin in town, because to my knowledge everyone else started years ago. I was saving myself, but for what? Now I may never know because it would mean begging this man to do the wicked deed and I would rather die than beg for something so… embarrassing.

I lie on my back and grip the sheet tightly to my body and listen out for any indication he sleeps. There is none and I lie like a frozen statue until somehow, against all the odds, I drift into a troubled sleep.

CHAPTER 13

TOBIAS

I wake early, as usual. However, for the first time in my life, I'm not alone. For a while, I just stare at my new bride. Her face has relaxed as she sleeps and as I watch her even breathing and the slight flush to her cheeks, I feel emotions I thought were lost to me. She seems so vulnerable and fragile and as if one touch could break her. Her blonde hair frames her face and those natural red lips are plump and desirable. She even bites them in her sleep, and my cock twitches with undisguised impatience. Last night didn't go as planned, and I have to remind myself to be patient. Good things come to those who wait, and she is definitely worth waiting for.

Last night she was angry, and rightly so. I did promise her own room and reneged on it. Not that I care about that. Her fate was sealed the moment I saw her in that dress, and now it's just a matter of time.

She stirs and whimpers in her sleep and the blood rushes to my head. What is she afraid of in her dreams? I'm surprised to discover I would do anything to chase it away and try to ignore the fact it could me she is dreaming of. I am a monster and I'm sure I feature in many a person's nightmares, but it unnerves me to think of starring in hers. I want to protect and care for her where nobody has before. This woman has awakened strange uncared for feelings inside me and I can't allow that.

Flipping on my back, I stare at the ceiling and curse myself for being a fool. What was I thinking? Sophia was right—as always. This marriage was a bad idea because far from being the marriage of convenience I wanted; it's threatening to undo all the good work I have done since…

Sliding out of the bed, I pace to the bathroom and stare at myself in the mirror. What I see is a fool staring back at me. Cursing, I run the tap and splash some water on my face and groan. Fucking idiot. How did I allow her in? Making a fist, I try to shake her out, but even I know she's there. Somehow, she's crawled into my black heart and let the light in. The trouble is, once the cracks begin to show, it's certain the rest of the structure will crumble unless something is done and fast.

Turning on the shower, I step naked into it and let the hot jets wash away my shame. I'm better than this. I'm stronger than this and with a sinking feeling I know what must be done. I need to push her out and it will be hard because I promised her a fucking honeymoon and now I'll have to revert to Plan B. Plan bastard because it's the only way I'll drive her out of my aching heart.

So, I dress and leave my sleeping beauty and head downstairs to get some much-needed distance between us.

As I reach the kitchen, Mrs. Billings looks up and nods respectfully.

"Good morning, sir."

I nod and take my seat at the table, which is laid for two,

and I snarl, "Make up a tray and take it upstairs for my wife. She won't be joining us."

She nods and if she thinks this unusual, she doesn't show it because she knows better than most how my moods swing like a pendulum.

Grabbing a glass of juice, I drink it almost in one and pick up my phone as Matteo enters.

"Good morning, Mr. Moretti."

I nod toward the chair opposite.

"Did you get my instructions?"

"Yes, sir."

"It's changed."

He remains silent and I snap. "The honeymoon's off. Call the airfield and have my plane made ready to leave in one hour. I need to head to New York to check on the Clarkson account."

Matteo nods and as usual his expression is blank but I know he will be forming his own conclusions why things have changed and I wonder what they are because even I don't know myself what's possessing me right now.

"You're up early."

Sophia slides into the seat next to me and reaches for the juice, looking at me with interest and I snap, "Go on, say it."

She leans back and regards me through her heavy lashes, and I swear I see a flash of disappointment in her eyes before she closes them and laughs softly. "Things didn't go as planned then."

"None of your business."

I help myself to a slice of toast and spread some butter and marmalade before attempting to eat something, but it turns to dust in my mouth. My appetite remains for only one thing and for my own sanity I need to leave it where it sleeps, because I've come to the conclusion it will ruin me forever.

Sophia says softly, "I'm sorry, Tobias."

"For what?"

"For the situation we're in. It's not right."

Feeling irritated, I snap, "For fuck's sake, it's 7am and I don't need a heart to heart with you. You've got what you wanted and now I'll have to deal with it."

"You're wrong."

"What?" I snap irritably and to my surprise, she reaches across and grips my hand tightly and says in a small voice. "I just want you to be happy."

Snatching it away, I say irritably, "Then get dressed, we leave in half an hour."

"Where are we going?"

"New York."

"Can't it wait?"

"No. I want to wrap this up because I'm done biding my time. I need Clarkson to man up and do the right thing."

"Which is?"

"Sell me his fucking company before I ruin him forever. I need a distraction and he is just what I need right now."

"And Anastasia? What about her?"

"Exactly. Now if you'll excuse me."

I scrape back my chair and she says in surprise, "What about your breakfast, you must eat?"

"I'm not hungry."

Before she can annoy me any further with her unwelcome conversation, I stride from the room and head upstairs to change. The sooner I get out of here, the better. I can't deal with what's here—not yet, anyway. I need some distance to set my heart back on track. Whatever this infatuation is stops now because if I allow her inside, it will destroy everything I've worked so hard to build and I can't let that happen.

∼

Exactly thirty minutes later, I step inside the car waiting outside and Sophia slides in beside me. Matteo jumps into the front and says into his headset, "We're ready."

The car in front pulls away and we soon follow with the car behind, bringing up the rear. As convoys go, this is a deadly one because I never travel alone. It's for our protection and has always been this way since the day my parents died.

Snapping open my briefcase, I remove the Clarkson file and handing the duplicate file to Sophia, we settle back for some all-important reading and I forget all about the woman who doesn't even know what she's done.

CHAPTER 14

ANASTASIA

He's gone. The space beside me is empty and cold and as I look around the infernally large room, I can see that I'm alone. Listening out for any signs of life, I just find an eerie quiet that unsettles me. Where is he?

Suddenly, the door opens to the suite and I hear the rustle of someone coming. Feeling a sudden flash of fear, I fully expect to see my new husband prowling toward me but am surprised when a thin, severe looking woman enters the room.

"Good morning, Mrs. Moretti. My name is Mrs. Billings, and I have been instructed to serve you breakfast."

"Um, good morning. That's very kind of you."

Swinging my legs out of the bed, I relish the feel of the soft pile carpet under my bare feet and walk with her to the small sitting room where I notice a table has been set for one overlooking the garden. I take a seat and she says politely, "Would you like some coffee?"

I nod and watch as she turns and pours some hot coffee into a delicate bone china cup and places it before me. "Creamer is on the table. I have brought you some toast and pastries to be starting with. I have some eggs, bacon and pancakes warming on the side but if you would prefer something else, I can make it for you."

Feeling a little uncomfortable, I say quickly, "No, that will be fine, thank you."

She nods and says respectfully, "If you need anything, the number is on the phone. Just lift the receiver and dial 5."

She turns to leave and I say quickly, "Um, thank you."

She nods and I say, "Um, excuse me, but will my husband be joining me?"

I almost see a flash of pity in her eyes before she shakes her head. "Mr. Moretti has left for a trip to New York. He will be gone for a couple of days."

"New York, but…"

I stare at her in astonishment, and she smiles thinly. "If you need anything while he's gone, I am here to serve, and he has left instructions you are not to leave the house. As I said, if you need anything at all, I am here to help."

This time as she turns away, I don't stop her because a burning knot of fury has formed inside me. He's gone to New York. What the fuck? I thought we were going on our honeymoon. What an asshole.

Angrily, I chew on my toast and look out over a garden that is the grandest I have ever seen. It stretches away into the distance and begs to be explored. In fact, this whole house is begging for my attention and I slowly settle down. He's gone. Maybe that's a good thing because it means I'm off the hook. Whatever he had planned for me has obviously been cast aside for something much more important and I should be relieved, but strangely, I'm not. If I feel anything, it's disappointment and feeling angry at that. I try to get a grip on my emotions. Surely this is what I wanted all the time, isn't it?

Despite everything, I am hungry and the food laid out for

me is delicious. So, I eat every last crumb and after several cups of coffee, feel ready to face my first day in my new home.

I decide to take my time in getting ready and just savor my unexpected privacy. My first stop is a long, hot shower, and this is one hundred percent luxury. Wrapping a large fluffy towel around my dripping body, I relish the heat it provides and sigh with satisfaction. I could get used to this.

I clean my teeth and comb out my hair and then head into my closet to dry it and select a suitable outfit for exploring.

It doesn't take long and I am soon dressed in jeans and a t-shirt with some leather flip flops on my feet. I wear no make-up because what's the point? I have the place to myself and I can't wait for that. Having lived under the shadow of my parents all my life, my days were never my own. They were always planned out for me with either study or music classes. In fact, I think I had every class going from extra tuition to language lessons and needlework. As I grew older, my time was volunteered to local charities and attending functions with my mom. I was her puppet, and that never changed when she arranged my engagement to Sebastian Stone. Then my job title changed, and I was expected to play the dutiful fiancée. I attended charity galas and coffee mornings and then at night was placed on his arm to attend business dinners and theater opening nights. We were the perfect couple in company and strangers when the car door shut. Much the same as now, and my heart sinks as I realize that the only thing that's changed is my address.

Once I'm ready, I head off to explore this amazing house, and it takes all morning to do so. Every room is impressive and decorated in a regency style that must have cost millions to create. I am in awe of the huge tapestries on the walls and the ornate gold leaf furniture and valuable looking antiques. Huge sweet-smelling flower arrangements delight me as I walk from room to room, and heavy fabrics hang proudly at the windows that show a stunning world outside.

The sun is shining and I open the huge doors of a particularly pretty sitting room and head out onto a patio that stretches the entire width of the house. There are steps down onto a manicured lawn and in the distance, I see a walled garden and tennis courts.

Happily, I set about exploring my new home and then look in surprise as I sense I'm being watched. Turning swiftly, I see a man watching me, his eyes disguised by the usual black sunglasses, and he is wearing the same suit the others all wear. He nods respectfully and I say in surprise, "Oh, I'm sorry, I didn't know you were there."

He heads toward me and says in a soft voice, "I'm sorry to startle you, Mrs. Moretti, I'm Angelo, Mr. Moretti has asked me to remain and make sure you have everything you need."

I stare at him in surprise. "Like what?"

He smiles briefly. "I am here if you have any questions and to keep you safe."

"Safe? Why, what could happen to me here?"

"Nothing ma'am."

I feel a little confused and then it dawns on me and I say bitterly, "What you mean is, you are here to make sure I stay, is that right?"

He says nothing, and I sigh. "So, if I asked you to arrange a car to take me to town, you would do it, right?"

"I'm sorry, Mrs. Moretti, that is not allowed."

"What about if I wanted you to take me to see my sister?"

"Mr. Moretti has asked that you remain here."

I feel slightly hysterical as I snap. "What, I can't even go and see my mom?"

"If Mr. Moretti agrees, that could be arranged."

"Then ask him."

"I'm sorry ma'am, but Mr. Moretti has asked not to be disturbed."

I feel the frustration building and snap, "Then get me his number and I'll call him."

He almost looks sorry for me and says gently, "Ma'am, Mr. Moretti has left strict instructions that he is not to be disturbed. He also made it clear that you are not to leave the house for any reason. I am afraid I can't help with any of your requests."

Turning away, I force myself not to shout and scream like a petulant child. It's ok for him to go heading off to New York, but I have to wait here like a discarded toy that he's bored playing with.

Sighing to myself, I say with resignation, "Am I allowed to call anyone at least?"

Angelo nods and reaches inside his pocket for a phone and offers it to me. "Of course."

Snatching it from his hands, I walk away and feel the tears building as I realize I have no one to call, anyway. I never really had that close friend you always thought you'd have. It was always Angel until my parents ruined our relationship by fixing me up with her boyfriend behind her back. I had many school friends, but they drifted off when school ended and I never made time for them. I will certainly not be calling mom and the only other person I can think of is Martha, so with shaking fingers, I dial my former home and sit on a nearby bench, desperate to hear a familiar loving voice.

"Good morning, The Johnson household."

"Martha."

My voice breaks as the feeling of relief overwhelms me when I hear her soft comforting voice.

"Anastasia, darling, how are you?"

"I'm struggling."

I can hear the concern in her voice as she whispers, *"I'm sorry to hear that."*

"It's so hard being away from home. It's all strange and nothing makes sense anymore."

"Don't worry, darling, it's natural, you've got quite a big adjustment to make."

"But what if I can't? What if I want to come home?"

There's a brief silence, and then she sighs.

"You have to give it time. Change is something that requires it. You have never lived outside these walls, honey, and it's natural to feel anxious. You're also living with strangers, which takes a lot of adjusting to. My advice would be to settle in and discover your new home and family. After a few days it won't seem so strange anymore and you will begin to feel at home."

"Home?" I laugh bitterly.

"That's the last thing I want to feel. You see, Martha, when I left, I wanted something more. I wanted to feel free where I never have before. I suppose I thought this was the answer to everything, but I've just swapped one lonely prison for another."

"What about your husband, maybe he can take you out somewhere?"

"I doubt it, you see, he left this morning and won't be back for a couple of days. I've been told to stay and wait for him, but I'm alone except for a housekeeper and a bodyguard. This sucks, Martha. I thought I'd have a life, you know, be free to do what normal people do, but I'm not."

"Then do what makes you happy, honey. Discover your new home and make it yours. You're married now and are the lady of the house, as they say. You have to make that job count for something and I'm sure Mr. Moretti would be pleased to see you're taking it seriously."

For a minute, I let her words register. Of course, this is

my home now, and she's right. I'm in charge, or at least I should be.

Feeling a little happier, I say softly, "Thanks Martha, I knew I could count on you to make me feel better."

"I'm always here for you, honey You know that."

The tears threaten to be my undoing once again, but I hold them back and say softly, "I love you, Martha."

Then I cut the call before she can reply because I can't deal with emotion right now. I need to harden my heart and take charge, and Tobias Moretti will just have to deal with what that involves.

CHAPTER 15

ANASTASIA

My first stop is to explore this amazing mansion. The only people who appear to be still here are my guardian devil and Mrs. Billings, and an eerie silence follows me wherever I go. With every room I discover, though, I fall in love with this place just a little more. Despite being the grandest house I have ever seen, it also has a warmness to it and provides a comfort that can't be described. Whoever designed this place knows their stuff because it could have turned out cold and unfeeling, but it isn't.

Little homey touches make it a home, and the stunning art and impressive furnishings make my eyes pop. There is nothing I would change, and it gives me hope for my time here. Maybe I could settle here. Tobias may travel a lot, and I would be free to enjoy the luxury this place provides.

The morning passes in a flash as I explore every inch of the palace I now call home.

One room in particular makes me laugh with delight because it lies on the topmost floor and the view across the gardens is stunning. I feel on top of the world in here, as the sunlight streams through the floor to ceiling window and lets nature into surely the prettiest room I have ever seen in my life.

It is decorated in the palest blue and the wallpaper is an intricate design of nature and birds that appear to be woven from silk. As I run my hand over it, I feel a softness to the material that warms my heart. The drapes are made out of the palest blue silk, interwoven with the same design as the walls, and they feel heavy and opulent. White scatter rugs provide a deep comforting tread and the huge bed that dominates the room faces the window and I sink back and appreciate the comfort the plump pillows and heavy comforter give me. I almost groan at the luxury and imagine myself reading here for most of the day as I lose myself in worlds that are exciting and captivate my imagination far more than ordinary life.

As I savor the luxury, an idea hits me and I feel a stirring of excitement. Tobias said that I had to stay with him, but he didn't say anything about when he is gone. I could make this my room and now the idea has taken hold, I look around with satisfaction. Yes, I will make this room mine, and if he won't give me my own space, I'll take it for myself.

Jumping to my feet, I feel a new determination. Yes, I will make this work. I won't play the victim like I've done all my life. I will make the best of a bad situation and Martha's right; I am the lady of the house now and I should have some authority here.

Feeling a lot better, I leave the gorgeous room, vowing to return later with my things and set up residence in a place I never dreamed of owning. Like Tobias, I like to own pretty things and this room is the start of that.

Humming to myself, I head off and continue exploring the immense space.

OWNING BEAUTY

∼

THE HOUSE APPEARS to be made up of four parts. North, South, East and West. Each has its own staircase and Tobias appears to occupy the East wing. This is the biggest part of the house, and the South and North wings appear to be smaller. The South is made up of various rooms that look as if he runs his business from here. A couple of the doors are locked, but the other rooms reveal its purpose. The feel to this wing is different to the rest of the house. It's pure business, and the wood paneling and antique desks creak with power. There are huge fireplaces in every room and amazing art that hangs with pride over them. The carpeting is deep and luxurious upstairs and in the more formal rooms and where it is not, are beautiful Italian marble floors that the underfloor heating makes pleasant on bare feet.

The North wing is made of up several other rooms that look to be occupied by the staff. There is a communal kitchen and living room, and many of the doors are locked. However, the ones that aren't, show a comfortable bedroom equipped with a bathroom and closet that must be home to the many people who work here.

Then I reach the West wing and find the door to the entrance locked. It appears to be out of bounds and I wonder about it.

Feeling curious, I head to the kitchen in search of the only other woman here and find her baking in the dream kitchen that I am itching to explore myself.

She looks up as I enter the room and nods. "Good afternoon, Mrs. Moretti, I have taken the trouble to provide lunch in the garden room if you are hungry."

She looks at me curiously and I smile my thanks and jump on the bar stool to watch her work. "Thanks, Mrs. Billings, that's very kind of you. Do you mind if I eat it in here? I'll run and help myself, but it would be good to have company."

She looks a little surprised and says quickly, "I will bring it to you."

"No, it's fine, I can fetch it."

"No madam, Mr. Moretti would not appreciate it. Please stay here and let me do my job."

She is rather curt and as I watch her head off with a hint of disapproval following her, my heart sinks. Great, now I've upset her. The tears burn as I think about the many times I sat watching Martha in the kitchen and wish she was here now instead of the rather cold, Mrs. Billings. She was such fun to be around and it makes me miss her even more.

In fact, despite being the most beautiful place I have ever seen, it is also the emptiest. The beauty is breath taking, but it has no heart. Much like its owner, I suppose and I giggle to myself. Yes, Tobias Moretti has modeled his house as he has modeled himself. Impressive, immaculate and so beautiful it hurts to look at it. However, inside is empty with a coldness that belies the exterior. Then again, there were little slivers of warmth that showed me the humanity inside the man, and it's those I cling onto as I wait for Mrs. Billings. Maybe it's in there somewhere and I have yet to discover the secret to breathing life into a black soul.

∼

Mrs. Billings soon returns with a lunch fit for a king. A silver tray groans under the weight of a beautifully prepared salad, with homemade rolls and a plate of cured meat. Fresh fruit and a sparkling wine accompany it and as she sets it before me, I can't wait to devour the contents.

She nods her appreciation as I tuck in and groan. "Mrs.

Billings, you are a wonder. This food is worthy of five Michelin stars. You are wasted here."

She smiles, which makes me almost stop eating because it completely transforms her features. As her face changes, the cool exterior lifts and I see a person that I much prefer emerging from the wall of ice she hides behind.

"You are very kind, Mrs. Moretti."

The sparkle in her eyes tells me she isn't often complimented on her work, and I feel sad for her.

As I eat, I watch and find it interesting to see her creating amazing food out of the ingredients she uses. Deciding to find out a little more about her, I say with interest, "Have you worked here long?"

"Five years."

"You deserve a medal."

She says nothing, but I see her lips twitch as she carries on kneading the bread she is making.

"Do you have a family, or a husband?"

She shakes her head and I see a wistful look enter her eyes. "My husband died five years ago."

She looks down and I can tell the subject is closed. "I'm so sorry, that must have been hard."

She nods, keeping her eyes lowered. "Is that when you came here?"

She turns and heads toward a cupboard to remove a baking sheet and says in a low voice, "Yes."

I feel a little bad for prying because it's obviously a subject she is uncomfortable with, but I want her to open up a little.

"It must get lonely, do you have any family to visit, or friends, clubs?"

She shakes her head and carries on with her work. "No."

Parking the conversation for another day, I let her off the

hook and say with interest, "This is a lovely home. You do a good job."

"Thank you, ma'am."

"Please, call me Ana, Mrs. Moretti is weird because I'm not sure who she is and my real name Anastasia is quite a mouthful, so my family and friends call me Ana."

She looks at me with a hint of disapproval. "I'm sorry, I have to address you by your title, it would be disrespectful of me not to."

Feeling frustrated, I vow to work on her a little and once again change the subject. "I've had such a great time exploring. There was one section of the house I couldn't get into, what's in there?"

"You must mean the West wing."

"Yes. the door was locked."

"It always is because that's where Miss. Moretti has her suite of rooms. The only ones with a key are the maids who clean it every day. They work solely for her and she guards her privacy well."

Thinking about the beautiful woman I met at the wedding, I feel a surge of interest toward my new sister-in-law.

"Tell me about her. I was introduced to her at the wedding, but we never actually spoke. What's she like?"

Once again, I see the woman's guarded expression close her down, and she says respectfully, "Miss. Moretti is a very private person. She lives here and works with Mr. Moretti. They run their businesses together and she is never from his side."

"Oh."

Thinking about their situation, it strikes me as a little odd. "Doesn't she have a family of her own, or a boyfriend perhaps?"

Mrs. Billings looks down and I see the pain cloud her

eyes, which instantly intrigues me.

"No, she has Mr. Moretti and until you came, he only had her."

Chewing on an apple, I think about their situation. Two siblings working and sharing a home is a little intense, and I wonder why. I can tell the subject is closed because Mrs. Billings moves away and starts to clear her work station and I know I won't get any more information from her.

Parking it for another day, I say brightly, "Would you let me do some baking?"

She looks up in surprise and astonishment, and I giggle. "Please, I love baking, cakes mainly and I'm itching to get my hands on this cooks dream of a kitchen. You can show me where everything is and I promise to clear up after."

"That won't be necessary, Mrs. Moretti, I will gladly help out."

She smiles and suddenly the wall of ice begins to thaw a little. Yes, slowly but surely, I will chip away and discover the secrets this house protects. After all, I certainly have the time.

TOBIAS

New York isn't helping. I came here to forget the woman I married in a misguided attempt to gain more control in my life and in doing so found the opposite. I am in danger of losing every ounce of control I possess around her and so came here to take my mind off my domestic situation and get back to business.

However, Sophia is withdrawn and angry and it's irritating me, and the Clarkson deal is stalling, which is stirring up a storm that I would rather do without.

As soon as we conclude our business with Jeffrey Clarkson, we head back to my Manhattan apartment, and Sophia immediately retires to her room. That's normal and any worries I have for my sister are once again buried in that box inside my head where I file away things I can't face.

My men take up their positions on the floor below, acting as a human shield to anyone who is foolish enough to think they can reach me and my sister, and the only person I have left is Matteo, who stands silently waiting for instruction.

As I stare out of the panoramic window at the city that never sleeps, I reach for the bottle of whiskey and stare moodily out on a place I own.

Below are the people I control through fear and intimidation. All across the city they do my work and I reap the rewards of it. Drugs, prostitution and gambling, I have shares in it in every city in America and increasingly it's infecting my soul with a poison that's killing me. Then there are the legitimate businesses I own that Sergio oversees for me, and I now have so many, I have lost count of them.

Sighing, I turn to Matteo and snap, "Call Ingrid and tell her to come."

He nods and leaves, and I immediately regret my words. Why did I ask for her? The woman I turn to when I head to the city. There are many of them across the country, and they serve my needs when required. I meet many women through my business who make no secret of the fact they want to be the next Mrs. Moretti. I am not interested and use these women to accompany me to functions and restaurants to keep the wannabees away. They make my life less complicated and ask for nothing but the money I give them, along with the lifestyle they crave, and they ask no questions and just wait for my call. Then I fuck them and they leave, no questions asked and no emotional attachment. Yes, I came here to set my life back on track. Anastasia is just one of *them*. A woman I pay to perform the role of my choosing, and I would be a fool to let her inside my black heart. She has a place, and it's time I cemented her in it.

Knocking back the liquid, it burns as it blazes a trail to my fucked-up soul, and I rip off my tie and shrug out of my jacket. Tomorrow I will finalize the Clarkson deal and will not take no for an answer. Tonight, I will fuck Anastasia out of my head and business will carry on as before.

However, as I wait, my thoughts return once more to home and I wonder what she thought when she woke up to find me gone. I expect she was angry, but then again, maybe she was happy to be let off the hook. Maybe she couldn't wait for me to leave. That thought leaves a bitter taste in my mouth, and I reach for another whiskey.

As I stare out across the city, I picture the woman I married and am instantly hard. There is something so appealing about Anastasia Johnson, and I can't put my finger on it.

Groaning, I sink down on the seat overlooking the city and put my head in my hands. Why can't I shake her? I must shake her because I can't develop feelings for anyone.

Twenty minutes later, the elevator pings and I straighten up. Yes, Ingrid will make those thoughts go away and as she walks into the room, I see the business in her eyes and my heart settles a little.

"Tobias."

She smiles and I see the lust on her face as the door clicks softly shut behind her.

I say nothing and just stare at her with my usual hunger, and she reaches behind her and pulls the zipper down on her dress. As she steps out, it reveals she has nothing on underneath and as I see the swell of the breasts that I paid for, my cock hardens. Licking her lips, she tosses her long, dark hair across her shoulder and walks suggestively toward me and then sinks to her knees.

Settling between my legs, she rubs my aching cock

against my trousers and purrs, "Let me deal with that for you, sir."

I nod, and she unzips my pants and frees the raging beast inside and licks her lips, her eyes flashing with greed. As she lowers her mouth and takes it all in, I relish the sound of her sucking and slurping as she sucks me deep and hard. Her tongue swirls against my shaft, and I thrust in deeper. I fist her hair and relish the bite as she feels the pain on her scalp. I thrust hard and deep and she gags as I punish her for not being the one I want, and I hear a whimper as I go too far and hold her head in place so she has no air.

Then the disgust hits me and I push her away, saying sharply, "Go."

She gasps for air and falls back on her ass and says fearfully, "Did I do something wrong?"

Feeling like a complete bastard, I zip up my pants and reach for my wallet, tossing a bunch of notes in her direction and snarl. "Take this and leave. I won't be needing you again."

She looks up at me with a mixture of hurt and anger and whimpers, "Please, tell me if I did something wrong."

Her pathetic groveling angers me more and I snarl. "I don't want you anymore, get out."

My eyes must warn her against any further explanation because she sobs and gathers her discarded clothing and leaves the room as quickly as she came.

Feeling frustrated, I hurl my glass against the wall and relish the sound of the glass shattering as I face up to my current situation.

I couldn't do it. I couldn't bear another woman near me because I only want one. Her. The frustration threatens to tear me apart, and I storm to my bathroom and rip the clothes from my body in haste. Then I stand under the powerful jets of water and take my cock in my hand and groan as I deal with it myself and every moment is imagining her mouth doing the job for me. I picture myself tasting her most intimate place and I imagine burying myself balls deep inside a little piece of heaven. Yes, Anastasia Johnson is so far inside my head, there is no way of getting her out but giving my cock what it wants. Until I sample the woman herself, I am ruined for all others.

As I come, I roar with release and understanding. I can't hide from the fact I am screwed and no amount of distance will get that woman out of my head, and I was a fool to think otherwise.

Placing my hands on the tiles of the shower, I try to get a grip. I must get a grip because I can't allow my infatuation with my new wife to destroy everything I've worked so hard for during the past five years.

There is only way to set things back on track and that's to fuck my wife senseless and then carry on with my day.

CHAPTER 16

ANASTASIA

I may not have my freedom outside of this house, but I am determined to find some inside. The afternoon is spent baking cakes and while they cool, I take a walk in the grounds, conscious of the discreet presence of Angelo shadowing my every move.

After a while, I turn and beckon him over and as he approaches nervously; I fix a determined look on my face. We are standing by a huge lake that is set some distance from the house. It is breath taking in its beauty, and I could stay here all day if I had to. I see in the distance a world I am no longer part of. In fact, it's as if I'm on another planet entirely because there is no view of another building, or person, as far as the eye can see.

Angelo hovers nervously nearby, and I say as gently as I can. "You know, you really don't need to follow me. I'm not going anywhere and I'm sure you have better things to do with your time."

"Excuse me, ma'am but I'm just doing my job."

I look at him with interest because Angelo is something else. He must be around late teens and has a wild look about him that the youth wear so well. Hell, he's not much younger than me and I wonder why he has chosen such a career.

I decide to see what makes Angelo tick and smile warmly. "Tell me, what made you apply for a job here?"

He looks at me in surprise. "I didn't."

"Then how come you work here."

He looks a little awkward and says softly, "It was always going to be my calling. My father worked for Mr. Moretti, man and boy, and it was always expected that I would too."

I stare at him in confusion. "Your father, how could he work for Mr. Moretti, the math doesn't add up."

Angelo looks awkward. "Mr. Moretti, senior."

"Oh."

I feel a little foolish because I never once considered Tobias had an actual family outside of his sister, and I wonder why he never mentions them.

"Where do they live?"

Now Angelo looks extremely uncomfortable and shakes his head. "I'm sorry ma'am, I'm not allowed to discuss personal family business."

I can feel the frustration tearing through my reasoning and snap, "I am family."

He nods, but even I know that sounded ridiculous. Of course, I'm not family. I'm a stranger brought in to do a job and he is reminding me of that. I'm not here through any other means than a business deal, and suddenly I feel weary.

Turning away, I say in a small voice, "That's fine, you may go."

He retreats to a respectful distance, but I know he's still watching me and I feel the tears burn. Is this my life? Am I to be watched silently, like a caged tiger in the zoo? I feel the chains of my new life tearing at my spirit. They are hurting my soul and I can't breathe. I thought I was marrying to get my freedom. How wrong could I be? All I've achieved is another kind of loneliness and have retreated into a world where normal life ceases to exist.

I can't deal with it and start running. I'm conscious of Angelo behind me and up my pace. My breath is torn from my body as it struggles to keep up as I run at speed around the lake as if I have a place to go. I am running from a life I never knew the consequences of, and I am running from the prison I now find myself occupying. I am also running from the bitter disappointment that I have sacrificed myself to an unfeeling monster who controls me when he has no business doing so.

If I feel any pity for Angelo, I push it away because he must be sweating buckets in that heavy black suit he's wearing. Still, I run because it offers me the only shred of freedom I have left and it's only when my body rebels and shuts down that I fall to my knees and welcome oblivion.

~

I OPEN my eyes because something cool is pressed to my face, and I see the anxious face of Mrs. Billings looking down on me. "Mrs. Moretti, can you hear me?"

I nod and as my eyes adjust, I see that I'm lying on a couch in the beautiful reception room overlooking the garden. Angelo is hovering nearby, looking so anxious I immediately feel guilty. I try to smile and laugh with a little embarrassment. "I'm so sorry, I don't know what came over me."

Mrs. Billings looks at me disapprovingly and shakes her head. "You overstretched yourself and passed out. Angelo carried you back to the house. I will call the family doctor."

"No."

I sit up sharply and feel like a fool. "I'm sorry, it was my fault, I pushed myself too hard."

I look across at Angelo and say apologetically, "Please forgive me. I acted like a spoiled child and never considered you at all. You must be exhausted. Please accept my apologies."

"There are none needed."

He half smiles and I feel bad. These poor people have been saddled with a grade A bitch, and I smile apologetically. "I'm sorry to be so much trouble, I'll try to behave."

Mrs. Billings shares a look with Angelo and he turns and leaves with a small smile and she sits beside me on the couch. I stare at her in surprise as she says gently. "Listen, my dear, you are going through a period of adjustment. You're far from home and lonely and have been left to deal with a situation that you can't get the measure of. Mr. Moretti is a difficult man, but not an unkind one. You would be hard pressed to find a better husband and any flaws in his character are there for a reason."

"What are those reasons, Mrs. Billings?"

I know she won't tell me because instantly her expression shifts and she faces me with a hard expression. "I am not at liberty to discuss my employer, or anyone else that lives under this roof. If you seek answers, there is only one place you will find them."

I sink back on the couch and feel so frustrated I want to scream. What is this place? There are so many secrets swirling around it, I almost can't breathe. The people here are extremely guarded, which makes me wonder why. There is something so devastating in the past that it's tainted the present. Maybe it's my job to make sure it doesn't do the same to my future, so I smile weakly and say in a small voice. "I think I'll go and have a lie down. Please can you thank Angelo for rescuing me, he must be exhausted?"

Mrs. Billings nods. "He's a good man. Don't make his job

difficult for him, Mrs. Moretti, because he will suffer the consequences of your actions."

She stands up stiffly and moves away, and I stare after her in shock. What does she mean, he will suffer the consequences of my actions? Surely Tobias isn't that much of a dick?

Feeling weary, I head out of the room and take the staircase to the East wing. However, I don't take the door leading to his bedroom but take the one leading to the pretty room I felt so at home in before. For a moment, I just stare out of the window at the immaculate garden and a lone tear falls down my face. Loneliness is a friend to me and the only one I've got. It's been walking with me side by side my entire life. Nothing has changed, just the scene out of my window and once again it's all I've got as I contemplate just the two of us in my depressing future.

So, loneliness and I snuggle down into the huge comfortable bed and wrap each other up in the familiar, as I close my eyes tightly and try to sleep off a situation that is starting to suffocate me.

CHAPTER 17

TOBIAS

We remain in New York for three days. I am impossible to be around and I know it. The anger has accompanied me everywhere, and even my men are starting to look anxious. Sophia knows to keep quiet when I'm in one of my moods, and conversation is strictly limited to business. She retreats to her room at the end of the day and I wonder what she finds to do in there because her life, like mine, is not a flexible one. She keeps herself to herself and only ventures out to accompany me on business and the odd function in the evening. She never complains but does remind me of what an asshole I am when needed. Yes, I need to keep my sister close because she's all I've got and we are both fearful of that changing, which is why we tolerate each other the way we do.

As we head to the private airfield where my jet is waiting, I feel the ache in my knuckles and know the bruising on my stomach must be quite impressive right now. Usually sex is my preferred release from the stress of the day, but as that appears not an option right now, I turned to my love of boxing to fill my evenings.

I own a gym down near Brooklyn and spent the last two nights fighting my frustration away. I love nothing more than smashing my opponent, and they kept a steady stream of unfortunates for me to play with. Men that have overstepped the mark were brought to the gym to face my own brand of punishment and were mainly carried off on a stretcher. I relish the power I feel when I hold a man's life in my hands and the battering they received at my hands pleased me way more than watching another put them in their place.

My men know I like to enact my own form of revenge from time to time, and as workouts go, this was a good trip. However, now I am keen to return home to deal with a different kind of problem and once again feel my cock hardening at the thought of what that means.

Sophia sighs and says in a dull voice. "You can't fight your way out of feeling all your life, Tobias."

"What are you talking about?" I say it irritably because we both know what she means.

"You, and your love of fighting. It's not healthy inside and out. You need to deal with your emotions differently brother because everyone can see you're losing your shit and that's not good for business."

"Shut the fuck up, you don't get to lecture me on the business."

"Is that so? Then tell me, brother, if not me, who? You see, you need a reality check from time to time and this existence is not healthy for either of us."

I stare out the window, hating that she's right. The trouble is, I can't change who I am, how I feel, or the situation we are now in because of what happened to them.

I feel on the edge and snap. "Don't lecture me. I'm fully aware of the current situation. What do you suggest, forget what happened and carry on living what is classed as a normal life for as long as they let me? Blend in with the rest of civilization as if we're not the cancer spreading through the country, responsible for most of the crime and drug addiction? Wake up Sophia and realize just what a shit storm we inherited because the only people who can change all this died five years ago."

She gasps as I make reference to the day our life changed forever and I turn away. I can feel her grief surround her as she battles to gather her emotions and keep them in check. She will hate that I have dared to disturb the tight seal she has placed on the box she shut the past inside and I feel like the bastard I am as I growl, "You don't lecture me on my behavior when you're as fucked up as I am. What's the matter, sis, don't you like the fact your brother keeps you safe because he actually cares what happens to you? Don't you like the life I created to keep you from suffering a similar fate and don't you like that I am trying to get some kind of normal into our lives that may just move us away from the fucked-up inheritance we have to live with because if you don't like any of that, you can leave, the door is open."

"Are you fucking kidding me? The door is open? Have you heard yourself? The door is most certainly not fucking open because you threw the key away. You stopped normal life getting in and you have created this vacuum we live in. If I leave, I know you will follow because you can't bear the thought of me escaping this fucked-up life beside your side. Don't lecture me on wanting something better because you have decided that better means dragging some poor innocent girl down to hell with you. Do the right thing and set her free because you won't like what sits on your conscience if you don't."

"ENOUGH!" My voice blasts through the car, causing it to swerve a little as the driver must hear it through the glass partitioned screen. "Don't you fucking lecture me. This is how it is until *I* decide otherwise and you will do as I say because…"

"Because what, Tobias? Because I may actually have a chance at happiness again, and you can't deal with it. Maybe I want that. Maybe I want to be set free to live a normal life with a husband and a family of my own. Why can't you see that?"

I turn away because I can't trust myself not to silence her in a way that would make me more of a monster than I am already. Sophia is my sister and gets away with a lot, more than anyone ever has because despite everything, I love her so hard it hurts and she is the only thing left for me to love. It's why she is a prisoner of my love, because if anything happened to my sister, the world would not be big enough for the person who hurt her to escape from me.

The rest of the journey home is spent in silence. My men avoid my eyes and Sophia positions herself at the back of the plane, as far away from me as she can get. The flight attendants share worried looks as I snap at them, and the air is thick with tension as I allow the drink to distort my vision of the man I have to face in the mirror.

The short drive back home is tense and silent, and I feel weary. The only light at the end of the tunnel is what's waiting for me. My little caged bird. The exotic beauty that I have locked in the tower to please me and entertain me at my own whim. Yes, her innocence and softness will be a welcome balm to take the sting away of a fraught few days. Tonight, I will set my future in place with her by my side, and it's that thought that's keeping me sane.

CHAPTER 18

ANASTASIA

Today has been better. I woke with a new purpose and decided to make the best of a bad situation. Dressing in comfortable clothes of some cut-off shorts and a tight vest, I put my hair in a high ponytail and once again leave my feet as bare as my face.

Today I intend on baking and exploring some more and feel quite upbeat for a change. Mrs. Billings is a little less frosty and Angelo keeps away all the while I'm inside the house, and I feel a sense of freedom that I never felt before. I can do this; I can carve a role for myself when he isn't here.

Mrs. Billings has resigned to sharing her kitchen with me, and we are soon chatting away like old friends. She passes on tips on baking, which I lap up eagerly. We have discovered a shared passion and I indulge it for most of the day.

We soon have quite the feast laid out before us and with excitement I call for Angelo.

He comes racing in looking worried, and I giggle as I point to the stool against the breakfast bar. "Sit there and be our Guinea pig."

He looks confused, and Mrs. Billings shakes her head and laughs at the startled look on his face.

"Come on, Angelo, we have been baking all morning and there is nobody around to eat it. So, what do you think of this brownie and tell me the truth, mind?"

I wink and pass the brownie across the counter and look with eagerness as he shrugs and puts some in his mouth. I love the way his eyes light up as he savors the flavor and nods, "Good ma'am."

"What about this flapjack?"

Once again, I pass him a small slice and he nods his approval. "You bake well, ma'am."

Feeling quite pleased with myself, I set about making him taste all my offerings, and Mrs. Billings laughs. "Poor Angelo, he will need to attack the gym after this, or we'll be letting his suit out."

We all laugh and then the happy atmosphere is killed stone dead as we hear, "Leave."

I see Angelo stand to attention and look uncomfortable as he turns to face Tobias, whose eyes are flashing dangerously as he watches us from the doorway. Mrs. Billings turns pale as she nods to Angelo and they head out of the kitchen with no words spoken.

I stare in surprise as Tobias prowls into the room looking so angry, I feel the fear ripping through my body as he snarls, "What are you wearing?"

Looking down at my cut-offs, I shrug. "Just what I normally wear around the house."

He growls. "Not my house, in front of my staff."

"Why?" I am genuinely confused, and he reaches out and pulls me sharply to him and snarls, "They can see everything and my wife is not a common slut. The shorts are too high, I can see your ass and that vest is clinging on for dear life."

If it was a shock at seeing him, it's an even greater one

feeling him touch me. I'm not sure why but it's as if my entire body comes alive and I'm absolutely mortified when he smirks and as my gaze follows his I see my nipples pressing hard against the thin fabric that contains them.

I feel my face flush as he stares at me with a hunger that sends the heat traveling through my entire body and he growls, "Did you miss me?"

I lick my lips nervously and his eyes darken to two flashing pools of electricity.

I can't breathe because he takes all the air in the room and replaces it with pressure. There is something about the wildness in his eyes that makes me quiver inside. He pulls me closer and anchors me to him like a snare and whispers darkly, "It's time to set some rules. Come with me."

Then he turns and pulls me behind him, and I struggle to keep up.

We pass his sister standing in the hall watching us, and something in her expression strikes fear in my heart. She looks frightened and I hear her say, "Tobias, stop. Don't do this."

He completely ignores her and the last thing I see is the apology in her eyes as she stares after me with a helplessness that fills me with fear. What's happening?

I don't have time to make sense of the situation as he pulls me toward the East wing and up the stairs to his bedroom. My heart is thumping so fast I can't keep up with it, and the fear is clouding my mind. He's scaring me.

Then, as we reach his room, he slams the bedroom door shut and pushes me down on the bed and stands over me, looking so feral I hold my breath and close my eyes because I don't want to see the look in his.

"Open your eyes."

His command is terse and brutal and doesn't tolerate delay, so I open them and shiver as he looks at me with overflowing lust. I start to tremble as he growls, "Things have changed. I no longer want a wife in name only."

"What do you mean?" My voice shakes as I stall for time, and he smiles darkly. "I'm sure you understand what's happening here. I came to a decision when I was away. I have forbidden you from other men, and it would be hypocritical if I screwed other women. So, that leaves the two of us and as your husband I want a wife in every sense of the word."

I edge back on the bed in fear because I am not ready for this. The sad fact is I am so turned on right now because I want this man so badly who does things to me inside that I have only read about. The trouble is, I'm not ready. I can't possibly entertain the idea because he will be disappointed when he realizes I know nothing at all about sex and everything that goes with it.

I swallow hard as he removes his shirt, and then I see the dark bruising covering his chest and gasp. "What happened?"

He looks down and shrugs. "The usual work out, it will pass."

I can't tear my eyes from it as the angry purple bruises cover the six pack of a man who is surely every woman's fantasy, and then it strikes me how weird this all is. I should be afraid and screaming for help. I should be shouting and pleading for him to stay away, and I should be crying and telling him to stop. But I have a morbid fascination with the man I married, and so I scoot forward and reach out and touch the bruises and feel him stiffen in surprise.

I raise my eyes to his and see his flash with a yearning for what I can give him, and it empowers me. As I lightly stroke his chest, he tenses and stills and I see the power I have over him. As I feel the nerves edging away, I bite my lower lip and he groans.

Now I know the power a woman has over a man, and I

get what everyone told me. This is an intoxicating game that I am loath to surrender.

I carry on exploring his body with a light touch and with every stroke, I get a reaction that spurs me on. I lick my lips with a nervous anticipation and say softly, "Let me put something on those bruises."

Shaking his head, he growls, "Leave them, they're fine."

Taking his hand, I notice the knuckles are split and grazed and I kiss each one of them as if to kiss the pain away. Once again, he groans, and it's as if I now hold all the cards. The lion is being tamed by the lioness, and it feels amazing.

With a new found authority to my voice, I say firmly, "Lie on the bed. I won't be long."

Unbelievably, he does as I say and I head to the bathroom and wet a cloth with cold water. Removing a tube of antiseptic cream from the medicine cupboard, I return and sit beside him and whisper, "Close your eyes."

His eyes shut and I apply the cream in soft stroking movements to his tortured skin, and he growls, "That feels so good."

"Shh."

Carefully, I apply the cold cloth and as he lies there, I appreciate the view without him looking. He is the finest man I have ever seen and despite being terrifying, under my touch he is like a pussy cat.

I carry on my administrations until all the tension leaves the room and as I pull away, his eyes open and a hand reaches out and grabs my wrist. "You're going nowhere."

He sits up and faces me and I can feel his breath on my face as he whispers in that husky, sexy voice, "My turn now."

He reaches for my vest and suddenly the danger is in the room again and I stare at him with a fear that I know irritates him because he strokes my face softly and whispers, "I'm not going to hurt you."

"But."

My voice trembles as I try to think of any excuse other than the real truth to make him stop, and his eyes narrow a fraction before he growls. "I repeat, I am not going to hurt you. That is the furthest thing from my mind. I want to give you pleasure; so much pleasure you won't be able to remember your own name. I want you to dream about me at night because even in your dreams, I want to be with you. I want to hear you scream my name as I send you to a place you will never want to leave, and I want my name to be the first one on your lips when you wake in the morning and the last one at night. I want to own every inch of you my little bird because I want you that much."

The power in his voice and the promise in his eyes set me on edge.

I am no match for this man. As soon as he samples the goods, he will wish he had chosen better. Struggling to breathe in this lust-filled atmosphere, I say with a quiver to my voice, "I'm a virgin."

CHAPTER 19

TOBIAS

*H*er words cause the blood to rush to my head and every part of me that she controls. A virgin - what the fuck?

I stare at her in surprise and she lowers her head as if ashamed. That angers me way too much and I lift her face to mine and say with choked emotion, "Is this true - how?"

She nods sadly and says in a small voice, "I never got the opportunity. Through school and college, I had many guys try, but I wanted to save myself for the right man. As I grew older, the opportunities went away because I was engaged to Sebastian, who never wanted me. I once tried to force him to love me by dressing up as a whore and visiting him in his office. I thought that's what women did, but he was disgusted."

The tears fill her lovely eyes and she turns away, leaving me ready to murder Sebastian Stone on sight. Then again, he has left me the most precious gift of all, and I should be thanking him for it.

Her shoulders shake as the tears fall, and I feel like the biggest bastard in the world as I see what nearly just happened. Sophia was right. The results of my actions would not sit well with me, so I pull down her top and hold her close and stroke her hair as if comforting a child because that's what she is. She has not progressed to a woman yet, and I will not be the one who makes that a bad memory.

She starts to cry softly, and it tears my heart out. I nearly ruined something so precious I couldn't live with myself if I carried it through. A virgin—fuck me, how did I get so lucky to find her. No other man has touched her most prized possession, and I will be the one to show her amazing it can be.

"You're disappointed in me."

"What?"

I pull back and see the hurt in her eyes, and it makes me crazy. "Of course, I'm not, how could I be?"

She sniffs. "Because you wanted a wife who would make you happy. Someone who could be everything you wished for and I don't measure up."

Now I'm angry and snap. "What the fuck are you talking about? Nobody can measure up to *you*. Do you know what you have just given me?"

"No." Her voice is a whisper and I say incredulously, "You have just made me the happiest man alive. You are untouched by any hand, and I want to be the man to make you a woman. That is the most precious gift a woman can give, and you have saved it for me."

As I stare at her, I brush aside the fact that's strictly not true. She hasn't saved it for me, she saved it for the man she fell in love with. Quite frankly, I doubt that was ever going to be me, but it sure as hell is now. But not here, not now, and not under these circumstances.

I lower my lips to within an inch of hers and say softly, "Relax, little bird. I won't be taking anything from you today. Pack your bags we're going on that honeymoon."

"But?" She looks up in surprise and I seize my chance and lower my lips to hers and taste the innocence for myself. She tastes of everything sweet in life, and now I know why I married her. Anastasia Johnson is going to save me and she doesn't even know it. I am going to give her the world and make her *my* world. Everything I do will be for this woman because suddenly she has given me meaning to my life and I want her beside me every step of the way. I don't love Anastasia, I own her and won't stop until she's mine, mind, body and soul. She is my new hobby, my new passion and my new vocation. She will have everything I can give her except my heart, because now I know what I want. To replace love in my heart with *her*. And by the end of it, she will never want to fucking leave me. Sophia was wrong about my intentions. I don't want to scare my little bird away. I just want to clip her wings so she can never fly away, even if she wanted to, and I will make it my life's work to not give her a reason to fly.

∼

I LEAVE her to pack and head downstairs in a surprisingly good mood. The black cloud has lifted and I shout for Matteo as soon as my foot hits the bottom step. As expected, he soon comes running and I say good naturedly, "The trip is back on again. Instruct my pilot, we need to refuel and are heading to the hideaway."

"And Miss. Moretti?"

"Tell her of my plans. She can come if she wants, but she can remain here if she prefers."

He nods and hurries off and I head to the kitchen, where I find Mrs. Billings trying hard not to look me in the eye. I know she will feel as if she's disappointed me, so I say in a softer voice, "We are leaving for seven days. My sister may stay, so make sure she has everything she needs. Call ahead and instruct the staff at the hideaway that we're coming and to make things ready."

"Of course, sir."

Then I head to the office quarters and take my position behind my desk. Lifting my phone, I call for Angelo and it isn't long before he comes running.

He looks worried and well he might because the sight of him laughing with my wife almost caused me to shoot him on the spot.

However, I know he would have been uncomfortable with the situation and so I say gruffly, "Just for the record, Angelo, I do not appreciate seeing my wife laughing with my guards when I am not home. If she tries to engage you in any activity, or conversation, you are to decline. Do I make myself clear?"

"Yes, Mr. Moretti, sir."

"Further, I understand you rescued her when she passed out at the lake, and I thank you for your assistance. Aside from that, you never touch her again unless it's saving her life. Do I make myself clear?"

"Yes, Mr. Moretti, sir."

"You have proven to be a loyal member of my organization, Angelo, and I see great promise in you, don't let my wife get in the way of that because I have no filter where it concerns her. Now, under the circumstances, I think you should take on a different role and you will be assigned to Miss. Moretti's staff with immediate effect."

I note the disappointment in his eyes, but that can't be helped. Anastasia is a desirable woman, and Angelo is a good-looking young man with raging hormones. I am just preventing any attachments forming and he needs to know his place.

"You may leave. Matteo will instruct you on your new role."

He nods, "Thank you, sir, I will not let you down."

As the door closes behind him, I try to shake the image of him laughing with Anastasia. The jealously that raced through my body was a powerful emotion that surprised me. When I saw her standing there in those fuck me shorts and tight vest, I was consumed by passion. I wanted to bend her over that fucking counter and sink balls deep into her ass for daring to wiggle it so suggestively in public. Thank god I didn't because I would find it hard to live with myself if I had. Now I know the one vital piece of information she withheld from me. A virgin. *My* little virgin. What a prize she has held onto for so long. I will be the only man to touch her in her lifetime, and that makes me even more protective and much more of a bastard as I contemplate owning her in every way.

CHAPTER 20

ANASTASIA

While I pack my case, I think about what just happened. That was so intense and yet surprising. One minute I was terrified and the next wanting something to happen that is long overdue by now. I fight back the feelings that are alien to me. I want to know what it feels like to be with such a man. Will it hurt? I expect so. Will he be disappointed in me, probably? But I'll be a woman and know the secret everyone else seems to know already. I will be one of them and share an intimacy with a man that I crave and terrifies me at the same time.

Suddenly, I'm aware I'm not alone and look up in surprise to see Tobias's sister Sophia standing in the doorway.

She is certainly stunning with her long dark hair and startling green eyes. She's wearing a green silk dress that brings out the color in them and is looking at me with a mixture of relief and curiosity.

"Please, forgive the intrusion, I just wanted to meet you properly."

"Hi." I feel a little shy and my greeting comes out in a

whisper and she smiles softly. "Don't be nervous around me, honey, because unlike my brother, I don't bite."

She looks around and rolls her eyes. "I don't come in here much, but it's typical, Tobias. The best of everything with nothing left to chance."

"I prefer the blue room next door."

She laughs. "He had that one specially designed for you."

"Me?" I stare at her in surprise and she nods. "When he decided to marry you, he had the room designed with you in mind. It was supposed to be your room, but I can see things changed. Are you ok with that?"

Feeling a little uncomfortable, I shrug and she says kindly. "Listen, if anyone knows my brother, it's me. He's obnoxious, rude, possessive and angry most of the time. However, underneath all that rage and angst, he's a decent guy who found himself in an impossible situation. He's prone to violent rages and you would do well to keep away from him when they occur."

Now I feel afraid, and she shakes her head sympathetically. "Maybe you can calm him down. I certainly hope so. I just wanted you to know I'm here for you. We walk in each other's footsteps around him, and he expects us to comply with all his demands. You on the home front and me through business. I am all he has in the way of family, so I'm going nowhere. You, on the other hand, may not last as long, so just a word of advice, don't make it easy on him."

"Why are you telling me this?"

I feel a little unnerved and she says in a detached voice. "Because he wants you more than anything right now, but he may soon get bored. Don't take it personally because I hope for your sake he does."

"Excuse me?" I feel shocked by her words and she says sadly, "I hope it works out for you, but he's a difficult man to work out. For instance, he likes to travel and even in New

York, the day after your wedding, he had one of his booty calls summoned to perform. I just wanted to say, whatever he tells you, take it with a pinch of salt because my brother has a sexual appetite that one woman will never cope with on her own."

I can taste the disappointment as her sharply loaded words hit home. He has already been with another woman. What was that all about when he told me he was going to stay true to me? I feel like such a fool and it must show because she says kindly, "Listen, I want to help. Just say the word and I can make it all go away. If you want out, I can arrange it. Never feel as if you're on your own because I know more than most what it's like to live with him. Don't let him win, Anastasia, you owe it yourself to be stronger than you ever thought possible."

She sighs and then turns away, saying as an aside, "Enjoy your honeymoon, I'll see you when you get back."

As she goes, she leaves me feeling like a fool. Of course, Tobias will want other women. Why would I be so stupid to think he would be happy with little old inexperienced me? We don't even know each other and even before the ink was dry on our wedding certificate, he was celebrating with another woman in a different city, leaving me kicking my heels in this gilded cage.

The tears burn like acid behind my eyes as I contemplate my life ahead. A rich man's toy and trophy wife. Way to go, Anastasia, you get the prize for being the biggest dumb fuck of the class.

~

As soon as I'm packed, I head to the shower and wash my tears away. I need to harden my heart because nothing is as it seems in this house. The Morettis are as cold as ice, and I thought my family was bad. They are something else, and I wonder if that's what power does to a person. Makes them invincible and above morality.

By the time I've changed into a pale blue trouser suit, I feel the nerves resurfacing. My hand shakes as I apply my make-up and brush my golden hair so it swirls around me like a fluffy cloud. I find some pale blue suede heels that compliment my suit and grab a matching leather purse from the shelf in my closet.

After a spray of perfume, I feel ready to face the man again and head downstairs, leaving my bags to be collected.

As I reach the bottom step, I see the usual cluster of men in black suits and look for Angelo among them. I feel bad for him because he was doing nothing wrong, but he isn't to be seen.

The men look down as I approach, and I wonder why. Walking past them, I head to the kitchen and see Mrs. Billings wiping the counter top and smile at the one person who makes me feel comfortable around here.

"Have you seen, Mr. Moretti?"

She shakes her head. "I think he was in his office. I'm sure he won't be long."

Taking a seat at the counter, I smile as she says sweetly, "Can I get you anything?"

"A coffee would be nice."

She turns and reaches for the coffee pot and I watch her pour the steaming liquid into a mug and top it up with creamer before pushing it toward me.

She doesn't offer any conversation and I sense a different kind of atmosphere in the house now they are back.

After a few minutes, Tobias heads into the room, and I shiver inside. He has changed into more casual clothing, of black jeans and a button down top. He is unshaven and his hair slightly wild and I can see the tattoos that intrigue me decorating his arms, which flex as he walks. My mouth waters at the sight of so much testosterone heading my way, and as he reaches me, he says softly, "Are you ready?"

I nod, and he holds out his hand and takes mine, squeezing it firmly. Then he anchors me to his side once again and says abruptly, "Sophia is remaining here. Make sure she doesn't do anything stupid."

Mrs. Billings nods, and I feel surprised as I follow him outside. What does he mean?

Once again, we step into the middle car and I watch as the men jump into the other ones. I say in surprise, "Are they coming too?"

"Of course."

Tobias grins wickedly, and I can see the promise in his eyes. He may have stopped himself earlier, but his intentions are crystal clear. This is a honeymoon in every sense of the word because it's written on his face clearly. My innocence is soon to be a thing of the past and, by the looks of things, it's happening tonight.

CHAPTER 21

TOBIAS

Sitting with my wife beside me is an experience I am enjoying way more than having my sister. She is quiet and withdrawn, and I expect it's due to what happened earlier. She must be nervous, so I squeeze her hand a little tighter because I want her to feel safe with me. For some reason I can't let go of her for a minute, which surprises me because I'm not one for affection. I usually enjoy women's company for only one thing and yet here I am, working out ways to make conversation with the one beside me so I don't scare her away.

After a while, she says a little nervously, "Where are we going exactly?"

"My island."

"Your what?"

She stares at me in surprise, and I laugh softly. "My island. I bought it a few years back as an escape. The only thing there is my island estate and I call it the hideaway."

She falls silent and don't ask me how I know, but I'm aware something has changed since the bedroom and it unnerves me. She's distant and pre-occupied, and I feel curious as to why.

Turning, I lift her face to mine and say firmly, "What's up?"

The flush to her cheeks tells me I was right and she won't look me in the eye. Gripping her face a little tighter, I say it again. "Answer me, what's up?"

Her beautiful blue eyes swirl with tortured feelings, and it disturbs me. I stare at her pointedly and she looks down and whispers, "Did your girlfriend from New York visit the island too?"

Immediately the rage floods through me and I hiss, "Who told you about her?"

I don't really need to know because it could only have been one person, and I say with a sigh. "Sophia."

She nods and I shrug as if it's of no consequence because it isn't. "I take no women there, especially not a whore." Her eyes widen and I laugh dully. "Maybe Sophia neglected to tell you the full story. Yes, I have many women who serve a purpose dotted across the country who are ready when I call. I pay them well for their time and that's all it is—business. When I went to New York, I needed to create some distance between us and called for Ingrid. However, the moment she took my cock in her mouth, I knew I was done with the lot of them."

She blushes and looks away, and I snap. "I told you it wouldn't be fair to you if I did the very thing I told you not to. It took Ingrid to make me realize that, so you should be thanking her. The fact Sophia told you, means I now have a problem with my sister, but I'll deal with her on our return. This is our honeymoon and you don't need to worry about other women because there aren't any and never have been. You are the first, my little bird. The first one I married. The first one who slept in my bed, hell who came to my home.

The first woman I have let inside my head and the first woman I am taking to the hideaway. You are also the first woman I have wanted to kiss so much it causes my heart to physically ache and you are the first woman I have bared my soul to. So, put any thoughts of other women out of your beautiful mind because the only thing I want you to think of is me and how much pleasure I can give you."

I watch in awe as my words hit home and she smiles suddenly, which takes my breath away. It's like a rainbow in the sunshine. The tears mixed with that smile cause something magical and I can't hold back and pull her lips to mine and punish them for ever doubting my intentions.

Feeling this woman trembling in my arms is too much, and I pull her tighter and bite her bottom lip that tempts me so often. She moans softly and my cock begs to be set free because she turns me on so much, I am tempted to pull her on my lap and take her right now.

But I practice restraint and pull away and love the way her lips are swollen and her eyes heavy with desire. Yes, my little caged bird is about to learn a valuable lesson, and I cannot wait to be the teacher.

~

We are soon at the airfield, and I watch with pleasure as she stares at the private jet in astonishment. "You own this?"

I nod with pride because this plane is one of my favorite toys. It stands there sleek and mean just like me and is emblazoned with my company logo and the corporate colors of my family.

As the car stops and the doors open, I take her hand and help her from the car. She blinks in the sunlight as she looks at the aircraft and I head up the steps, pulling her proudly behind me.

The flight attendant beams her welcome and looks at Anastasia with interest. Yes, today is a day for firsts because aside from my sister, I have never taken a woman on board my private jet.

I love her reaction to my plane. Her eyes sparkle with excitement as she looks at the interior of the executive jet. Like my homes, I spared no expense and the plush seats and deep pile carpet tell the observer they are in the lap of luxury.

My men crowd on board, and I make sure that Anastasia sits next to me at the front and the attendant hands us a glass of champagne. "Congratulations Mr. and Mrs. Moretti, the crew wishes you a long and happy life together."

Anastasia smiles her thanks and something about the way her face lights up as she says thank you makes something shift inside me.

Her ring sparkles on her finger, and the heavy band of gold that accompanies it makes my heart swell with pride. She's mine—all mine, and I can't quite believe my luck. I never thought it would feel this good. I thought she would just wait for me at home to be wheeled out when needed. I certainly never expected her to share my bed, and I definitely never had a honeymoon in mind. This marriage is full of surprises and I like them. Life is certainly a lot more interesting with her around and I settle back in my seat and hope this plane can travel at supersonic speed because I can't get to the hideaway quickly enough.

CHAPTER 22

ANASTASIA

It's all a bit overwhelming. *He* is overwhelming and this jet, well, it's something else. I always knew he was rich, but never on this scale. Who the hell owns an island and a private jet? Tobias Moretti certainly does, which makes me wonder why he's so interested in me and Johnson's plastics. We must be just a drop in a very large ocean where his empire is concerned. He could have any woman he wants, and yet he chose me—why?

The flight attendants can't do enough for us, and the food and drink they serve is comparable to any in a fine restaurant. Tobias appears more relaxed than I have ever seen him and even the fact he has so many guards behind him ceases to matter and I almost forget they are there and the job they do.

Tobias is good company and talks about the places he has visited across the world in this aircraft, and I am a willing listener. It sounds so exciting and worlds away from my own upbringing and life to this point, and the excitement stirs as I think about how different my future is shaping up to be.

Then there's the man himself, and I can't quite believe my

luck. I never thought I would marry such a man, and I am excited to see what that means. The entire journey is torture because there is a physical ache inside as I contemplate our arrival and the events that will follow.

Am I ready for Tobias Moretti and his attention because the thought of it is making the heat tear through my body and a strange wetness between my legs? I'm almost worried it will be visible when I stand up, so I excuse myself and head to the small toilet on board the aircraft.

I feel mortified as I clean myself up and note the heightened flush to my cheeks and the wild look in my eye. What is happening to me? I don't recognize the person staring back at me in the mirror. This person appears to have changed overnight and I like what I see. I like what I feel and am impatient to see where this journey ends.

∾

BY THE TIME WE LAND, I am beyond excited. We are met at the steps of the aircraft by another fleet of cars, and we wait for the guards to set everything in place before we thank the crew and slide into the middle car.

I look out with interest on a tropical paradise and say with excitement, "Is this your island?"

Tobias shakes his head. "No, it's too small to land an aircraft on. We need to take a boat, but it's not far."

Once again, the excitement is almost too much—a boat. Another first.

He smiles at the excitement in my eyes and I say with a slightly nervous giggle, "Wow, today is a day of firsts for sure. My first private plane and my first boat, not to mention my first private island."

Suddenly, his eyes darken with desire and he leans

forward and whispers huskily, "I have reserved the best for later."

He kisses me softly and I melt into him because now I can't seem to get enough of feeling his lips on mine. However, this time it's different because it's not enough. I want more and I'm starting to realize the power of attraction.

When we reach the boat, I stare at it in astonishment and say, "Wow, some boat. It's more like a ship."

As we stand on the dock, I look at a huge power boat that stands proudly a short way out from the marina. It has its own berth and is easily the biggest boat here, and Tobias grips my hand and says with pride, "This is the Island Star. It can sleep 16 and is what is classed as a super-yacht. Occasionally, I like to vacation on here, but today it's merely a taxi service. Maybe next time we will experience the delights it offers, but not now."

I stare up at it in awe and almost have to pinch myself. Do people really live like this—do *I* really live like this? It's almost too much and I fall silent as I follow him onboard. For some reason, it is all starting to overwhelm me. How can I measure up and be the wife he needs? Surely, he will wake up tomorrow and realize his mistake because this is all well out of my league.

Again, we are met by a respectful crew who look at me with interest. I wonder if they can see what is obvious to me, that I'm on borrowed time here?

It doesn't take long for our belongings and the guards to settle on board, and soon the engines burst into life and we are on our way.

Tobias gives me a tour of the boat, and with every step I take, I feel even more nervous. It's all a little too much and when we arrive in the main cabin, I swallow hard as I see the enormous round bed that dominates a suite of rooms that rivals the one at the mansion and I feel dizzy with nerves. What if I disappoint him?

There's that nagging doubt at the back of my mind as I contemplate what will happen very soon. Will he look at me with the same disgust as Sebastian when I went to his office that day dressed as a whore? If he did, it would destroy me because the most surprising thing of all is that I am starting to develop actual feelings for my new husband, which means I'm totally screwed because a man like that doesn't have feelings. Of that I'm certain, so I bite my lip and fall silent as I feel totally out of my depth, both physically and mentally.

Tobias must notice a change in me because he looks concerned and pulls me close and stares into my eyes with questions burning in his.

"Is something bothering you, little bird?"

"It's nothing." I look down and once again, he forces my face to look at his and says ominously, "Never look away from me, I need to see your beautiful face."

Shaking a little, I say nervously, "I want to speak to my sister. I'm feeling a little overwhelmed by it all and need to talk to someone."

He looks taken aback, which surprises me, and then nods, and points to a phone by the side of the bed. "You can use that. I'll be on deck when you have finished."

He turns and leaves and I feel a little concerned because it was obvious he wasn't happy about my request.

However, I can't think about that and head across and sit gingerly on the bed and reach for the phone.

As I dial the number, I wonder if this was such a good idea. I'm feeling strange and hearing a familiar voice may change everything. However, the minute I hear her voice, a wave of homesickness washes over me as she says, *"Angel Johnson."*

"It's me, Ana."

"Oh my god, Ana, I've been so worried, why didn't you call?"

Swallowing hard, I try to battle my emotions and say lightly, "I'm sorry, I should have, but things have been so hectic I haven't had time."

"Where are you, is he treating you right, for fuck's sake, Ana, tell me because I've been scared shitless for you?"

I smile inside because Angel returned from where she's been a totally different person from the one who left. She's much harder and rough around the edges, probably because she lived with bikers for most of it. It's her strength I need right now, so I say a little more firmly, "It's amazing, Angel. Tobias lives like a king and you will never believe where I am now."

"Where?"

"On a super-yacht heading for his private island. We flew here in his private jet and I am so out of my depth, I'm worried."

Her sharp intake of breath makes me smile as she shouts, *"Oh my god, that's insane. I can't believe it. Have you got your cell, take some photos and send them to me, you have got to be kidding?"*

Hearing the excitement in her voice settles my nerves a little and then I say nervously, "The thing is, I need some advice."

"Like what?"

It's a little embarrassing and I almost can't say it but I take a deep breath and say nervously, "I'm still a virgin, Angel, and I'm scared about… well, you know?"

There is a sudden silence on the line and I wonder if we've been cut off and then she says in a softer voice, *"Oh honey, I never knew."*

Feeling the tears prick behind my eyes, I feel like such a failure. Then she says in a gentle tone, *"Do you want to have sex with Tobias?"*

I feel the embarrassment creeping over me and say in a small voice, "Yes."

"And he's treating you well?"

"Yes."

"But I thought it was a business arrangement, what changed?"

"Good question." I sigh heavily. "I suppose he's different from what I imagined. He seems, kinder and not so scary. He has surprised me and well…"

She laughs softly. *"And he's incredibly hot, that always helps."*

"Yes, just a little."

She giggles and I can't help but join her and my heart settles. Yes, I should have called Angel sooner because she is and always was the only one I could talk to.

Then she says smoothly, *"Don't overthink it. You know in your heart when you're ready and your body kind of takes over. Follow his lead and if I'm guessing right, he will know what to do. Don't worry and just lie back and enjoy the ride."*

She giggles. *"Let him direct the show because I'm sure he'll take charge, anyway. You know, honey, the fact you've called shows me you've changed. We haven't been close for a while and we both know the reasons for that. But I want my sister back and so, as soon as you get back, call me and we'll arrange to meet. I want to be here for you this time and if anyone knows what it's been like for you up to this point, it's me."*

A warm feeling spreads through me as my life settles back in place. Yes, I'm not alone anymore. I have Angel and Martha and for my sins, my mother. Now I have Tobias too, and that is what excites me the most. So, I push any doubts I may have down inside and say brightly, "Thanks, I feel better already. Send Martha my love, I miss her."

"Of course."

"What about mom, have you seen her since the wedding?"

"Not if I can help it. Martha told me she's out most nights,

anyway. I expect she's looking for husband number two because if I know our mom, she won't play at being the merry widow for long."

"I feel sorry for the man who falls for her lies."

Angel laughs. *"That's his problem because the less I have to do with Mirabelle Johnson, the better."*

She sighs and then says in a softer voice, *"Take care of yourself, honey. Remember, you have me and you always will. Don't be a stranger."*

"I won't and Angel…"

"Yes, honey."

"I love you."

I cut the call before she can reply, and the tears threaten to pull me under again. I meant what I said though, I do love my sister and feel upset that it's taken me until now to realize that. There is a lot of water under our particular bridge and I am just glad we came out the other side.

So, with a new found confidence knowing I'm not alone anymore, I head off to find my husband.

CHAPTER 23

TOBIAS

When I leave Anastasia in my cabin, I am tempted to listen in on her conversation. It angers me to think she is holding something back. I know she is because I felt it. Maybe she's having second thoughts about the whole situation? Perhaps she is dreading what comes next and wants her sister to help her escape. My thoughts take a dark turn and my earlier good mood evaporates as I head to the top deck to grab a much-needed whiskey. I don't like what she is doing to me. I'm like a jealous high school kid who can't control his woman. That's not me. I don't let them in, and she is testing my limits. I know I'm a jealous bastard, but I didn't realize just how much until her.

I see Matteo and a couple of the guys leaning against the rail and head across to them. They straighten up when they see me coming and I say gruffly, "Anything to tell me?"

They look to Matteo, who shakes his head. "No sign of Carlos and Sergio called to say the portfolio is shaping up well given the current situation on the markets. He will email you his report by the end of the day."

"Back to Carlos. How is he lying so low? Do you think he's dead already?"

The men share a look and Santi pipes up, "If he was dead, we would know about it. Word is out he's got a price on his head and for that sum of money even his own mother…"

He breaks off and looks down, realizing what he's said, and I sigh irritably. "That's in the past, it's the future that counts and he's a loose cannon. I want you to put word out to double the effort. I want every rock lifted that he could have crawled behind because that man has a target on his back and I want to be the one to hit it."

The guys nod and Matteo says sharply, "Miss. Moretti."

"What about her?"

"Is she safe left behind?"

"You tell me, Matteo." I fix him with a dark look and notice he looks uncomfortable. "You see, the men guarding her are *your* men. Do you not think they are up to the job?"

He squirms a little and nods. "Of course, but she can be…"

"I know what my sister can be, and it's up to you to manage that. Double her security and leave instructions she is not to leave the house. She's safe there and I hardly think seven days in the lap of luxury is a bad thing in her case."

Matteo nods and then I see Anastasia heading out into the sunlight and immediately my mood shifts to her.

Fixing my men with a black look, I snap, "Deal with it." before I head across and look for the answers I seek in those beautiful blue eyes.

However, when I reach her, I see something I never expected to see—lust.

I almost take a step back and she leans toward me and whispers, "Thank you."

"For what?"

"For letting me speak to my sister. I just needed to run a few things by her and she put my mind at rest."

Suddenly, I feel like a first-class fool. I should have known. She was drowning under the weight of responsibility because of everything I've shown her today. I'm guessing she feels a little out of her depth, but she couldn't be further from the truth. I'm the one floundering in an unknown sea, and yet my heart lifts as I see the genuine desire reflected back at me.

I almost can't believe such a creature wants me but apparently, she does, it's written all over her face and I am impatient to sample the pleasures that she's kept hidden for so long.

Reaching out, I take a strand of her hair and make a decision. It begins now. Here on the Island Star. By my reckoning we have an hour to kill and I can think of nothing I'd like more than spending it exploring this exquisite creature.

So, I lean down and whisper, "Are you ready for your first lesson?"

The sudden spark of desire in her eyes is a good answer, and I almost pull her over in my haste to reach my cabin.

It doesn't take long and soon we are right back where we were last and as I close and lock the door; I turn and regard the object of my fascination standing trembling before me.

She bites her lip and I feel my cock twitch as I say darkly, "Remove your jacket."

She faces me and does what I say, and I feel a rush of power surge through me. I imagine her on her knees and willing to do anything to please me. I remove my shirt and watch her pupils dilate and say gently, "Come to me."

She walks across the room nervously and as she reaches me, I take her hand and raise it to my lips, kissing it gently. She gasps and I love how the slightest thing turns her on and reaching for her satin top that she wore under her jacket, I pull it gently off, marveling at the way her breasts heave in the lacey bra that cost a small fortune. Those breasts are not man made, they are man desired, and I lower my lips to kiss the soft plump swell of her breasts as they heave before me. She gasps, and I feel her tense as I run my hand around the back and unfasten the catch, allowing them to spill free toward my eager hand. I touch them reverently, running my hand around the nipple, and relish the sight of it hardening under my touch. Lowering my lips, I take one in my mouth and roll my tongue around the tip, gently sucking as she moans against me.

Then I kiss a trail to her neck and bite gently, causing her to shake in my arms, and I love every minute of it. Exploring my wife is the best feeling in the world and I'm in no hurry, despite what my cock thinks.

Reaching for her, I unfasten her trousers and as they fall to her ankles, I lift her and carry her to the bed, dressed only in the palest blue lace panties.

As I settle her back against the plumped pillows, I take a moment to stare at the creature I have trapped in my lair. She is perfect and as she tries to cover her nakedness, I growl, "Do not try to hide from me. If you do, I will secure your wrists to the bed."

She gasps and yet I see a spark of desire light up her eyes and I laugh to myself. Interesting. Maybe my little innocent virgin will not be averse to my own particular pleasure. But not now. Now is all about creating something so wonderful she will crave recreating it every hour of the day.

My gaze travels all over her as I openly stare with unhidden lust at the creature quivering beneath me.

Keeping my jeans on, I kneel before her and gently ease those panties down before holding them to my face and sniff, savoring the scent of lust mixed with innocence. I can feel the beast in me roaring to devour her, but I hold it back. Not now. It's all about her and what she needs because I will not rush this moment.

Gently, I part her legs with my hands and lower my mouth to the place I have been desiring to go since I first laid eyes on this beauty many months ago.

I flick my tongue to taste the slick wet juices of her desire and she whimpers. Gently, I take her clit in my mouth and roll my tongue against it, gently nipping, causing friction and she moans. I can taste her desire and it spurs me on to lap like a greedy animal at the feet of a goddess.

She starts to wriggle and I smile against the hottest pussy I've had the pleasure to taste. She tastes so much better than any before her, reinforcing the decision I made. She is mine and I am the only man in the world who has tasted this piece of heaven and it makes me more feral than I was before.

As she writhes and gasps under my tongue, I feel how much she wants me. Like a new flower coming into bloom, she opens up to me and I can't get enough. Then she can't hold on much longer and her screams go straight to my heart because it's the scream of pleasure and discovering a whole new world. Anastasia Johnson is almost a woman, and I can't wait to explore the rest of her when we reach the island.

CHAPTER 24

ANASTASIA

I almost can't look at Tobias as I dress. What just happened? It was so embarrassing afterward but so intoxicating as he did things to me I would never admit to anyone else. Do people really do that? I'm not naïve and have heard about it but that - the feelings that he created were so incredible it's now my new favorite drug.

I hated the fact he watched me dress like a tiger stalking its prey. There is no getting away from him, and the thought that I screamed so loudly makes the heat travel through me again. What if anyone heard?

I quickly cover my modesty and almost can't look at him until he says firmly, "Come to me, little bird."

I do as he says with my eyes lowered and to my surprise, he fists my hair and pulls my head back to look up into his dark, flashing eyes. I wince as I feel the pain and he growls, "I said, never look down and always look people in the eye. You are a strong woman and I will not tolerate weakness around me."

I feel my eyes well with tears and fight them back. Then he grinds his lips to mine and begins an onslaught on my senses that leaves my lips bruised, swollen, and desperate for more. What is it about this man that terrifies me one minute and has me craving him the next?

He pulls away and strokes my hair with a gentleness that is the total opposite to what just happened and he whispers softly, "I have much to teach you and your fear is the first flaw we must deal with. You have nothing to fear from me, and I do not expect to see it in your eyes. You look at me as an equal and somebody who will always have your best interests at heart. I will not tolerate weakness, and if I see it again, I will punish you for it. Do you understand me?"

I gasp, "Yes, Tobias."

He leans in and growls. "Yes, sir, when I am teaching you a lesson."

"Um, yes, sir."

He releases me and then takes my hand and smiles. "Then the first lesson is concluded. I hope that has taken the embarrassment away."

Thinking of what he just did to me makes me smile, and he laughs. "When we reach the island, we will progress to the next one, immediately."

He winks and pulls me from the cabin, and I follow him in shock. I don't understand this man at all. One minute he's soft and gentle and the next hard and brutal. His moods switch like a pendulum and far from feeling confused, I just feel excited by it. I love both sides of him because one balances the other. It makes things exciting and I can't wait to see what else he has in store for me because as days go, this one is shaping up to be best one of my life.

THE ISLAND STAR is an incredible boat. The rest of the voyage is spent exploring and trying to come to terms with my new life. The entire time Tobias holds my hand and points things out that he thinks will interest me and obviously takes great pleasure from my excitement.

The staff keep a respectful distance and the guards are all but invisible to me now.

When he wants to be, Tobias is an engaging companion and today he is more relaxed than I have seen him before.

Soon we see land and he stands beside me at the prow of the boat and points to a white sandy beach, not far away. He says with pride, "The boat will drop anchor here and we will take the tender to the shore. The men will organize the luggage and the boat will wait for our return."

I feel so excited I can't speak because I have never seen such a place. We never traveled because my father didn't believe in it. He was a workaholic, and any vacations were spent in the area or at home. I feel as if my sheltered upbringing has impeded me, which was one of the reasons I agreed to this marriage. I want to explore the world. I want to see places I've read about, or seen on the television, or in movies. I want to sample different cuisine and shop in exotic locations. I want to feel the sun on my skin and gasp at a stunning sunrise, or watch the setting sun. There is so much I want to do, and Tobias can offer me that. In fact, the more I get to know him, the more I realize just what he can offer me, and suddenly my marriage becomes a little less scary and a lot more interesting.

We make our way to shore and I love the speed at which we travel across the waves. I feel the spray on my face and taste the saltiness of the droplets of water that catch on my lips. Tobias smiles as he watches me laugh as the spray hits me and I can tell my happiness pleases him. For some reason, I feel more relaxed around him and am keen to see where this new found understanding takes us.

The boat moors on a wooden jetty, and I see a party of

about six people lined up to greet us. Tobias jumps out first and then takes my hand, helping me exit the boat as gracefully as possible and I smile as a beaming woman dressed in a beautiful pink silk dress, hands me what appears to be a brightly decorated cocktail and says happily, "Welcome to the hideaway Mrs. Moretti."

She offers one to Tobias and says respectfully, "Welcome home, Mr. Moretti."

He takes the drink and actually smiles at her and says warmly, "Thank you, Marla. It's good to be here."

We shake the hands of the rest of the staff whose names I can't possibly remember, and we follow Marla toward the most breath-taking property I think I've ever seen. It shines like a jewel in a very golden crown and appears serene and calm and a place to forget normal life exists. Beautiful flowers are everywhere and white sails provide shade from the burning sun, under which are large double daybeds with deep white cushions begging for attention. I am blown away by this place and say in awe, "You are so lucky Tobias, this place is paradise."

He laughs softly, but I can tell he is pleased by my enthusiasm, because his obvious love of this house is plain to see.

"Come, I'll show you around."

He turns to Marla. "We will catch up later, Marla, I need some time with Mrs. Moretti first."

She almost bows and backs away and I stare after her in astonishment and he laughs. "Come."

Once again, I get a tour of luxury and each room is more incredible than the last. I can see why it's called the hideaway because there is nothing on the horizon, just open space and this serene piece of paradise that is ours to enjoy.

There are several pools of varying sizes and a couple of hot tubs depending on which way the sun is hitting. As properties go, this one is surely the most decadent and I wonder about the man I married. How rich is he for god's sake because no man should have this much wealth?

We reach the bedroom and I swallow hard as I see the stark white interior facing the ocean. There is a wall of glass separating us from the view and the bed is dressed in the purest white silk with just a few scatter cushions and white furniture to hold the bedside lamps, which provide a splash of color to an otherwise calm and peaceful space.

Tobias is obviously happy here and reaches out and swings me around with a lightness I haven't seen before, and it's contagious as I fall into fits of the giggles as we tumble onto the bed.

He rolls on top of me and says huskily, "Now is a good time for lesson number two."

Immediately, I feel a surge of lust and remember to look him in the eye. I almost close them again because suddenly he is serious and by the look of him, ready to play hard.

I feel a little anxious because anybody could see us and he must sense this because he whispers, "Relax, this side of the island is out of bounds. The only thing to watch us would be a lone sea bird, so relax and let me start the lesson.

I nod and he stands and says firmly, "Undress me."

Scooting off the bed, I reach for his shirt and lift it gently over his head, marveling at the abs of steel that are turning a more normal color now.

I long to kiss those bad boy tattoos and he growls, "It's yours, do whatever you want."

Leaning forward, I inhale the musky scent of the man who is fast becoming everything to me and then lick his nipple gently. He tenses and yet stands still and feeling more confident, I kiss him all over that infernally hard chest. "Now my pants."

With trembling fingers, I unbuckle his belt and hesitate as I reach the button fastening them closed. He growls with impatience and I can see why, because his pants are filling up and it must be uncomfortable for him, so I quickly pull down the zip and release his manhood from their confined space. Even through the thin fabric of his boxers, I see the sheer size of it and feel a little faint as I contemplate what he will use it for.

Then I slide his trousers down his legs and whimper as I see the full force of the man I am expected to take.

"The rest."

His voice is firm but I detect a rawness to it that tells me he's so turned on right now and with shaking fingers, I grip the waistband of his boxers and pull them down, almost afraid to look.

However, he is not having that and says roughly, "Look at me."

I look up and he has a wicked glint in his eye as he says roughly, "Stroke it."

Nervously, I reach out and find it's surprisingly smooth to touch and not at all unpleasant. As I caress the skin, he groans, and it begins to leak a thin white liquid from the tip. I feel a little concerned and look up, only for him to say roughly, "Now lick the tip."

Feeling quite sick at the thought, I can tell he is in no mood for me to refuse, so I gather any strength left in me and run my tongue over the tip and taste the saltiness of the man holding himself so still before me.

"Now take it in your mouth."

I feel curious but not disgusted and find I am eager to comply. As he slides to the back of my throat, I gag a little and he eases back, giving me room to adjust to him being inside my mouth.

He holds onto my head with both hands and says huskily, "I'm going to move now and you must suck as I push. Understand?"

I nod and as he starts to thrust forward, I try to suck and lick his velvet shaft as he completely fills my mouth. His grunts of pleasure spur me on and I find a strange fascination with making him groan even louder. If anyone could see us, they would see me fully dressed on my knees before this man as he punishes my mouth with hard, angry thrusts. He growls, "Grab my balls and squeeze them hard." Tentatively, I reach up and hold his testicles in my hand and slowly rotate them and he grunts. He increases his rhythm and I almost can't keep up as he thrusts into me like a man possessed. Despite this feeling a little degrading, I also find it extremely erotic and find myself daring to tease and lick him to make him groan even louder. I use my other hand to rub the base of his cock and apply a pressure that makes him roar. Then he grabs my head and thrusts in and out so quickly I almost gag and he roars, "You will swallow every drop."

Before I can even understand what he means, a thick salty liquid hits the back of my throat making me gag and he holds my head still and says roughly, "I said drink it."

Screwing my eyes tightly shut, I do as he asks and after the first drop slides down my throat, I relax and discover it's not that unpleasant. Then he pulls back and lifts me to him and holds me so tenderly, whispering, "Good girl. That was the best one ever."

I feel a surge of pride because I did that. I made him happy, and I thought I could never do it. He may have told me what to do, but I made him orgasm so hard, I'm sure they heard us back home.

Pulling back, he says softly, "Come, we will shower together."

Immediately, I tense and he shakes his head. "You will do as I say because by the time I take your virginity, there will be no barriers between us and you will be begging me to."

Trying so hard to act cool and as if I'm ok with all this, I smile shakily and he leans in and kisses me softly on the lips. "It's ok, my little bird, it's ok to feel shy and embarrassed. You don't have to pretend around me. I am here to teach you something amazing and I want you to realize just how powerful you are. Never be ashamed of what we do because it's the most natural thing in the world."

He kisses me so softly and sweetly it erases the fear from earlier. I almost believe he loves me because he is being so sweet and tender. Maybe he does, maybe I stand a chance of the happily ever after. Perhaps this is the start of a love affair that will last for eternity. I can only hope it is because now I've found him, I never want to let him go.

CHAPTER 25

TOBIAS

*A*nastasia is surprising me. I am enjoying her company and not just because I'm getting off on teaching her about sex. In fact, *I'm* surprising myself because normally I'm keen to just fuck a woman and be done with it, but this is proving quite the eye opener.

Watching her explore something so new and fantastic is opening my own eyes. I am relishing my role as her teacher and find myself wanting to give her so much pleasure, more than my own. That alone is unusual, and I wonder if it's just because it's different. It must be because I'm not one for patience.

Then again, she angers me when she fears me. It's like a knife cutting me inside when I see the pain and fear in her eyes. I want her to trust me. To open up and let me in. I don't want a woman who cowers away in a corner, fearful of what I may do. I know I'm not an easy man to tolerate, but sometimes she makes me feel as if I'm the devil incarnate.

As I lead her to the shower, I decide to tone it down a little. She needs nurturing, not frightening and for the first time in my life; I decide to put a woman first. I don't want to scare her away because I'm not certain I will let her go. That alone worries me because I made a vow to let no one in. It's why I've lived as I do. But now…

Feeling a little out of sorts, I break my promise to myself as quickly as I made it and revert back to the bully in me and snap, "Take off your clothes."

Her eyes widen and yet she does as I say and once again, I find myself hard for her. I'm not sure why, but this beauty has the ability to control me by one look alone and it's not what I want, so I decide to take back control as I'm used to doing.

She stands quivering before me, waiting for my command and my world rights itself.

She just stares at me as I instructed her to do, and I move toward her and reward her with a soft kiss. As I inhale the scent of a woman that appears to be a gift from God, I ignore the crashing of my heart and my nerves set on edge. I ignore the fact I want to please her so much, and I turn my back on what I know I should do.

Instead, I turn her slowly to face the screen and press her against the glass. Then I spread her legs and bend to kiss her neck and say gruffly, "Never be ashamed of your body my love, you have the most perfect one I have ever seen and now I want to taste every inch of it."

She shivers as I taste every part of her, by starting at her neck and moving my way down, until I reach the part of her I crave to be inside. Slipping my finger through her folds, I rub her clit until she moans. Pressing my shaft against her, she whimpers as the need overwhelms her.

I whisper, "What do you want?"

She says nothing and I say louder, "Answer me!"

She says in a small voice, "I don't know?"

I continue to rub her clit and love the way she gasps and trembles under my hand. I feel so powerful as I hold her innocence in my hand, and it takes all my strength to hold back. It's as if I can smell her fear, and it both excites and repulses me at the same time.

Spinning her around, I stare into her eyes and note the uncertainty in hers. Then I kiss her softly and gently, and she melts against my body as I settle between her legs. I gently rub against her and she presses her body against mine, desperate for something she doesn't know the power of.

Then I kiss a trail over her breasts, still massaging her clit, holding her on the edge of oblivion. Her juices flow against my fingers, and I know she is ready, but I need her to beg first.

As I run my tongue over the length of her clit, she shudders and I say, "Tell me."

I know she is fighting against her shame and it's important she learns how to communicate with me. She grasps my hair as I lick and tease her clit, and she struggles to understand what's happening. Then I pull away and she looks at me with surprise as I say firmly. "You have to beg if you want me to finish what I started. Do you want me to make you a woman, my darling?"

Her eyes are dilated and her breathing fast, and it's a beautiful sight to see. A woman on the edge of ecstasy, in unknown territory, and mine for the taking.

She nods and I say gruffly, "I said beg."

I can tell she is mortified but wants this so much she can't say no and she slowly nods and whispers, "Please, I'm begging you, Tobias."

The wicked bastard in me pulls her close and says roughly, "What do you want me to do, my little one?"

"Make love to me, Tobias."

Instantly, I freeze because I can't give her what she wants. How can I? I never promised her love. I promised to fuck her, not love her.

She must sense my retreat because she opens her eyes and the sight of the hurt in them causes something to shift inside and I pull her close and say huskily, "Beg me to fuck you."

If she is disappointed, she hides it well because she nods, "Fuck me, Tobias, I'm begging you."

That's all I needed to hear, and I sweep her into my arms and carry her to the bedroom. The shower can wait because I'm done waiting. As she lies underneath me, her eyes are wide with fear and I say soothingly, "This may hurt but only for a minute, do you trust me, little bird?"

She nods and I see her fear mixed with anticipation. She is so ready and as I take her mouth in mine, I kiss her with a soul searing kiss that causes my mind to explode. I am about to fuck my wife for the very first time, and I have never felt like this before.

She trembles underneath me and it sends me wild with lust as I kiss every inch of this beautiful creature to savor the moment. She starts to pant and pleads, "Please, I want you to fuck me, Tobias."

She is using my language, but it leaves me with a hollow feeling inside and I wonder why. She arches her back toward me and I try to shake off the feelings that are flooding my world. This isn't happening.

As she presses against me, I lose my mind and poise at the entrance to paradise. Then, with a growl, I position myself and feel her slick juices ready to ease me inside. She needs this, *I* need this if we are going to make this work, so I whisper, "I'm going to stretch you and it will hurt but stay with me and it will soon pass."

Her eyes are wide as she nods, and the trust in her eyes causes an explosion in my chest. I feel so protective over her and so I inch in carefully, waiting until her walls stretch to accommodate me before I probe deeper. She winces as I reach the barrier that's kept her mine and then with a sharp

OWNING BEAUTY

thrust, I break through and claim my woman. She gasps and the tears pour down her face as she bites her lip and yet I know it's a necessary pain. Stroking her hair, I whisper soothing words of encouragement before slowly moving back and then thrusting forward again, gently and carefully. Soon nature takes over and her body starts to adapt to the intrusion and I feel her relax as my cock finds its rhythm. I stroke her G-spot inside and she moans, and this time they are ones of passion. Reaching down, I pull her ass hard against me and she is as close to me as any woman has ever been. I stretch and tease her, taking care not to hurt her any more than I have to, and soon her cries are ones of passion as the pressure builds.

When Anastasia comes apart on my cock, my world changes forever. Now I know what it feels like to possess a woman fully and without compromise. As I enter her, she enters my mind, body and soul and we are cemented together for eternity because as I roar my release into the woman who has captured the beast, I know I will never want another woman. She is going nowhere.

CHAPTER 26

ANASTASIA

It hurts so badly and yet the feeling of Tobias inside me was amazing. I feel different now as I lie in the arms of my husband after he has taken away something I protected for so long. He is still inside me and as we lie joined together; I feel so happy that I finally know the secret that everyone else knew some time ago.

He whispers huskily, "Are you hurting?"

"A little."

I look up at him and his eyes are dancing with an expression I haven't seen in them before. He kisses my lips softly and whispers, "Thank you."

"What do you mean?"

"Thank you for giving yourself to me."

I bury my face in his chest and feel amazed that I'm here at all. This hasn't quite turned out how I thought it would, and yet I'm not complaining.

I feel a little stupid that I asked him to make love to me. We both know love doesn't come into this relationship and I push down the part of me that's disappointed about that. So, I don't have the love story - I have the dream and what a dream this is turning out to be. Maybe Tobias and I can just be good friends, who fuck. Yes, friends with benefits because we have to forge some kind of relationship out of this marriage. Maybe it will be fun to spend our evenings when he's home doing this, and when he's not, I will occupy my time another way. Yes, I need to work out a role for myself and this is just the icing on the cake.

He pulls back and looks a little anxious. "I'm going to pull out now and then run you a bath. It may be sore for a while and the hot water will help ease the pain."

I nod, suddenly fearful of what comes next and as he pulls out; I feel the burn a little, and then all that's left is a sore feeling below.

He rolls off the bed, and I stare at his masculine beauty as he heads toward the bathroom, and soon I hear the sound of the bath running and try to move. It feels as if I'm on fire and when I look down, I cry out because the blood staining the sheets makes it look as if there's been a stabbing.

Tobias comes running in. "What?"

I feel my face flame as he looks at the blood and grins. "In the past the bedsheets were paraded through the streets when a man claimed his bride, it was tradition to prove she was a virgin on her wedding day."

I stare at him in shock. "Yuk, that's so embarrassing."

He grins. "Like I said, no need to be embarrassed around me."

He comes and sits on the edge of the bed and tucks a stray piece of hair behind my ear and says somewhat apologetically, "I know this is a little irrelevant now, but have you been taking the contraceptive pill I arranged for you?"

I look down because that alone was the most embarrassing moment of my life when my mom announced he had sent them and I was to start taking them immediately under the terms of our contract.

He lifts my face to his and says darkly, "Well?"

I nod. "Of course, I followed your contract to the letter. Contraception - check. Prenuptial agreement signed. Permission to sign my name regarding Johnson's Plastics - check. Full medical and background - check. I did it all, Tobias, you know that."

I feel a little hurt that he would bring that up now, almost as if he's regretting what we just did and for a moment he seems at a loss, so I say slightly angrily, "Anyway, if you don't mind, I think I'd like some privacy to clean myself up."

I don't look at him, or wait for an answer and just head to the bathroom and shut the door, hoping he doesn't come in because as I'm becoming accustomed to, the bastard doesn't believe in locks on the doors.

As I sink into the hot, sweet smelling water of a bath that overlooks the ocean, I wince as my tortured body feels the burn.

Then I lie back and relish the view, marveling that I lost my virginity in such an island paradise.

Then I think of him and feel conflicted. On the one hand, what just happened was so magical and the perfect place and time for this to happen. He has been so kind and attentive all day, but then he had to go and ruin it by asking me to fuck him and then make sure I was on the pill. It made me feel like a cheap whore and the tears start to form as the disappointment bites. Then I feel foolish because what did I expect? Hearts and flowers and a declaration of love. I doubt the man has it in him, so I fight my disappointment and just concentrate on the positives instead. I did it. I finally did it and despite everything, it felt fucking amazing.

∽

I TAKE my time in the bath because it feels so good and the view is like nothing I've seen before. I'm not worried about keeping Tobias waiting because his actions have annoyed me. He turned something so magical on its head, and I will probably never forgive him for that. Then again, who was I kidding? He is hardly Romeo to my Juliet.

So, with a sigh, I dry myself off and grab a robe that's hanging behind the door. Feeling my skin glowing and not just from the bath, I smile as I feel different somehow. I have an inner peace that's the result of discarding my virginity and despite everything, I wouldn't change a thing of how it happened.

When I head into the bedroom, Tobias is waiting and sitting on the edge of the bed that now has no sheet. He looks up and I see conflict in his eyes as he says gently, "Hey, do you feel ok?"

I nod and smile. "Better thanks."

He pats the space beside him, which takes me back to our first meeting and despite wanting to tell him to go to hell, I do as he says because by the looks of him, he has something on his mind.

As I take my position, he reaches out and entwines his fingers with mine. "I'm sorry, Ana."

I blink because to my knowledge, this is the first time he's called me by the shortened version of my name, and it feels nice. More familiar and less formal.

"For what?"

"The comment about the contraception, asking you to use the word fuck instead of love, in fact making you feel something you shouldn't."

I stare at him in total surprise, and he shrugs. "I'm not good with words and I'm not good with feelings. I'm in unknown territory here and am asking you to cut me some slack. What just happened was the best sex I've ever had, and

I want you to know that. Nobody else has ever come close to that, so as a first attempt, I think you hit the jackpot."

I'm not sure what to say and just stare at him in total surprise, and he smiles gently. "I've taken the liberty and arranged a meal to be delivered to the beach outside. I'm not interested in seeing anyone this evening and just want to spend it with you. If you agree, that is."

How does he do this? Make me so mad with him one minute and the next, falling for him a little more. I swear he has a dual personality, and how could I refuse him anything when he is being so charming now?

So, I just nod and the relief in his expression says it all. "Ok, I'll jump in the shower while you make yourself comfortable. I won't be long."

He heads off quickly, leaving me completely baffled behind him. Was that an apology? It certainly seemed like it and for the first time since I met him, I discover an emotion I haven't felt before—hope.

CHAPTER 27

TOBIAS

I'm such a fucking idiot. As the steam from the shower burns my shame away, I try to get my head back in the game. As soon as I saw the look in her eyes when I mentioned the contraception, I knew it had come out the wrong way.

The trouble is, I'm not prepared to face the real reason I asked. I never wanted this. Hell, I tried all my life to avoid it but it's hit me like a sledgehammer. When I ran her bath, the overwhelming feeling I had was of fear. Fear that the woman who had given me so much would wake up one day and realize she doesn't need me anymore. She is wealthy in her own right and certainly doesn't need my money. A few weeks with me and she'll realize what a fucked-up bastard I am and pack her bags.

When I came inside Anastasia, it was not by accident because it hit me when I was inside her that I never wanted her to leave. I need her to stay with me, so I did something I never thought I'd do. I shot my seed so deep inside her; I hoped it would hit home. I want my baby planted firmly in her belly to chain her to me forever.

Now my own instructions in that god damned contract have come back to bite me because I have given her the protection against me she needs. Anastasia will wake up one day soon and discover she doesn't want me or this fucked-up life, and there is nothing I can do about it.

I knew she was angry and left her to her bath in peace, even though it tore me apart not to go in there and tell her how I really feel. But I can't. How can I admit something to her that I don't understand myself? I can't explain something I don't want or need in my life. Why I suddenly want a family goes against everything I said and if Sophia were here, she would laugh fit to burst.

Do I love Ana? It certainly feels that way, or is it just because of what just happened?

Groaning, I hit the tiles with my fist and sink to the floor; the water cascading over me washing away my shame. Somehow, somewhere in this fucked-up marriage, I actually developed feelings for the woman I wanted to possess Now who's the dumb fuck?

I arranged the dinner because I'm a greedy bastard and not for food. I want her all to myself and any person interrupting us for a minute is an irritation I'm not allowing to happen. No, this is a special night for us both, and I need to make things right between us, but I don't know how. Every time I open my mouth, the wrong words come out and I don't know how to say what I really want without looking like a complete and utter dickhead.

Feelings - I have run from them all my life and after what happened, vowed never to be in that position again. Now I am, I don't know what to do, so I gather my inner bastard around me and grab a robe and head back to see if I can somehow work it out as I go along.

As I walk into the room, Anastasia turns and the sight of her against the backdrop of the sea causes me to smile. She looks so happy as she says with excitement, "I always knew there was a beautiful world out there. I wanted to see it for myself and now I have, thank you."

"Have you never seen the ocean before?"

I find it hard to believe, but she nods. "No. My parents weren't one to travel and Angel and me just spent vacations at home with Martha. When I was older, I was still living at home and continued to do what they wanted. When they told me I had to marry Sebastian, I put everything into making that work."

She smiles, but the burning rage inside me won't go away as I think about how she has been used by the people who should have done everything in their power to make her happy.

"Well, you can travel the world now, little bird. You have your own wings and I will take you wherever you wish to go."

She stares at me for a moment and I see a spark of hope enter her eye. "Really?"

My heart physically aches as I see the pleasure in her smile and I say with a determination I know won't waver, "Anywhere, just name it and we'll go."

The phone rings by the bed and I grab it quickly. "Yes."

"Sir, your table is ready."

"Thank you, we'll be right there."

She looks at me with surprise and I reach for her hand. "Come, dinner is served and you must be hungry."

"Should we change?" She looks down at her robe and I feel the heat tearing through me as I picture her naked under it. "No, we will be alone. We can go naked if we want to."

The blush that creeps across her face makes me smile, and

before I make a complete asshole of myself, I pull her outside the bifold doors and down to the beach below.

As we walk barefoot in the sand, she gasps with pleasure. The sun is beginning to set over the horizon and the light show is fantastic. In front of us is a small table with a white tablecloth on top of which stands a candelabra lighting up a feast for a king and his queen. A bottle of champagne cools in the ice bucket next to it and as I hold out her chair, she smiles and whispers, "Thank you, Tobias, this is perfect."

Taking my seat opposite, I pour the champagne and raise mine in a toast. "To a long and happy marriage."

She looks surprised and then touches my glass with hers and says sweetly, "I second that."

I stare at her in fascination as she sips the champagne and try to push down the direction my thoughts are heading. Reaching for the plate of oysters, I hold one to her lips and say firmly, "Open your mouth."

She looks a little disgusted and I laugh to myself and then say sternly, "I said open your mouth."

She rolls her eyes and does as I say, and I tip the delicacy down her throat and love the way her eyes widen as she samples the treat.

"What did you think?"

"I'm not sure."

I take another and slip it down my throat and feel the pleasure it gives my taste buds. "Another one then."

She looks a little doubtful but to her credit, opens her mouth to allow me to pour another one down her throat and this time she nods. "Better."

"It always is when you get used to it." I grin and she giggles adorably, and I feel my cock throbbing. How does she do it? I've been with hundreds of women and none of them have affected me in the slightest, yet this woman, an inexperienced virgin, has done the unthinkable.

Snapping out of it, I reach for a spoon of caviar and hold it to her lips. "Open."

She pulls a face and says shortly, "Are you really going to feed me all night?"

"Yes."

"Why?"

"Because it gives me pleasure."

"What about me? Don't I get a say in it?"

I wink. "No."

I hold out the spoon and she opens her mouth and I watch her taste the expensive delicacy and her eyes shine. "That I like."

She takes a swig of the champagne and leans back, her robe falling open just a little, exposing the swell of her breast.

Once again, my cock begs to reach her and I say gruffly, "Come with me."

She looks up in surprise and I take her hand and place her champagne in the other one. "Come, we will drink this at the water's edge."

We walk hand in hand along the beach, sipping our champagne as the moon rises and there is nothing but the crash of the waves to disturb the peace. When we reach the edge of the waves, I place the glasses on the sand and stand before her. Then I ease her robe from her shoulders until she is standing naked before me, looking like a goddess in the moonlight. To her credit, she stands tall and without shame, and I allow my robe to join hers on the sand at my feet. Then I pull her close and kiss her like a lover would and relish the fact she melts into me and moans her pleasure.

Then I pull back and say gently, "Tell me."

"What?" Her voice is but a whisper.

"What do you want me to do?"

Without hesitation, she says, "Fuck me, Tobias."

I shake my head. "No."

She steps back and looks at me with a worried expression and I run my thumb over those lips that appear to have been created for my pleasure and say huskily, "Ask me to make love to you."

Her eyes fill with tears and she blinks them away and says softly, "Make love to me, Tobias."

Her words make my heart lift this time because they are what I want to hear. Yes, I must practice what I preach and face my fear because I am fast realizing that love is a vital ingredient in any relationship and that is what will bind her to my side forever. I could have all the riches in the world, but they would count for nothing if love wasn't a part of that.

So, I kiss my wife with love in my heart and the feelings inside me are intensified. As I press her body to the sand, I savor the woman who feels as if she was sent from God to be by my side. Then I kiss her all over and worship her like she deserves and when she can't take anymore, I inch inside her for the second time and wish I could stay here forever.

CHAPTER 28

ANASTASIA

Once again, Tobias has surprised me. When he made love to me on the sand under the moonlight, I gave him more than just my body. He now owns my heart. I am starting to understand him a little more because when he apologized; I saw him struggling, like me, in an unknown place. Maybe there is hope for us after all and I am now determined to try at least.

When I wake in the morning, it's wrapped in his arms. The sunlight replaces the moonlight and streams through the window, signifying the start of a glorious new day. Tobias is sleeping soundly, and I smile to myself. He is so handsome and all mine. I know that now because he told me again and again as we made love for most of the night. Now I know what it's like to have it all. He is everything and I will make it my life's work to make him happy.

He stirs and I trace the contours of his face softly and he opens his eyes and smiles. "That feels nice."

I say nothing and just lean in and kiss his lips softly and lightly, and he tenses under my touch. I feel him hard against me and smile.

He pulls me closer and growls, "Time for lesson number four."

"Only four, I thought surely we must be on lesson ten or eleven by now."

He grins wickedly and shakes his head.

"No, I'm pretty sure we were just going over it again and again. If I remember rightly, we never reached lesson number four."

Immediately the desire grips me and I feel the wetness between my legs. How my body craves this man, and he appears insatiable. Sophia was right. He has a sexual appetite that could keep me busy all day, but I'm happy about that.

He rolls me on top of him and I look into his eyes and smile, loving the way his breath hitches. Reaching up, he strokes my face reverently and whispers, "So beautiful. My goddess."

Then he growls, "I want you to sit on me, all the way in."

He pushes me up so I straddle his body and lifts me slightly, bringing me down onto his hard cock, and as it slides in, I gasp with pure pleasure. Then he growls, "Now ride my cock and own it, it's yours."

Feeling empowered, I start to move slowly at first and watch his expression change to one of pure pleasure as I squeeze his cock between my thighs. The friction builds as I drag my clit against his hard shaft, and I close my eyes, allowing the waves of ecstasy to build.

He growls, "Look at me."

Snapping my eyes open, I stare into the dark eyes filled with desire that gives me power and I speed up until my breasts bounce and he groans. "Harder."

I do as he says and move like a woman possessed by the devil as I buck on top of him and feel him invade me completely.

He grabs my arms and holds me firmly as he thrusts

inside me and his grunts of pleasure spur me on even faster. The pressure is too intense and I scream as my orgasm is torn from me by one powerful thrust and as his roar of release joins mine, I feel him throb inside me as he coats me with his seed.

I am out of breath and out of my mind as I look him in the eye and whisper, "I love you."

He freezes and looks at me in shock, and I know I've made a terrible mistake when he shuts down before my eyes.

Lifting me off him, he swings his legs to the side of the bed and growls, "Wait there."

Feeling confused and so mortified, I lean back and wonder what part of my crazy brain thought that was a good idea. He doesn't love me; it was in his eyes, and now I've ruined what we were building. He immediately withdrew from me mentally and physically and I feel like such a fool.

Wrapping the sheet around me, I walk across to the window and stare emotionlessly at the waves crashing to the shore. Way to go, Anastasia, ruin a good thing with one sentence.

I can see his reflection in the glass as he heads into the room, wearing a towel slung around his waist and looking as if someone just died. My heart is in my mouth as I sense change coming and know I won't like what I hear.

He moves behind me and wraps his arms around me and says huskily, "I'm sorry, you took me by surprise."

I say nothing and just let him talk because the fact I can't see his eyes is probably a good thing for both of us.

"I'm sorry, my darling, but I told you that being married to me would mean a life without love. I will give you the world and everything you could want, but I won't give you that."

A lone tear falls from my eye as I feel my own heart breaking. He did warn me, I suppose, but I thought…

He nuzzles my neck and whispers, "It's not that I don't want to, I can't. You see, I made a vow to myself years ago that I would never allow myself to love another person. You see, my love destroys. It taints what's good and like a cancer eats away at it until it's dead. Sophia is my blood, and we are two of a kind. We don't feel anymore—we have learned not to because when you love someone, when you allow them inside your head and your heart, they destroy you. Trust me, you will not want me to love you because my love is the devil's love and you will burn in hell with me. Understand that my little bird because I will not allow myself to love another as long as I live."

His words do not comfort me. They destroy the last shred of hope I had in me for a normal life.

Turning to face him, I say sadly, "Then I feel sorry for you, Tobias. You are missing out on the only thing in life that can bring you great happiness. You may have it all, good looks, wealth and a life no normal person could ever understand, but you are poorer for it because you won't allow yourself to open up and let someone in. You asked me if I could live without love because you could. I said I had lived without it all my life and now I'm not so sure."

His expression hardens as I shake my head sadly. "It's ok, we made a deal and I'm not one to go back on my word. Just maybe we should go back to how it was before either of us gets hurt."

I see a flash of pain in his eyes as he hisses, "Is that what you want?"

Turning away, I say sadly, "No, it's not but like you, I must do what's best for me and I can't allow myself to fall more in love with you because, as you said, it would destroy me. What happened here, on this magical island, will always be special to me because you showed me how amazing love can be if you let it. Thanks for that, but I must protect myself from allowing myself to hope for more. So, I will be your wife in public and in private under the terms of our contract, but I will not allow myself to love you."

I walk away with the tears streaming down my face as my world ends. Once again, I am chained to a relationship where the other person doesn't want me for the person I am inside, and only for what I can give them. When will I ever learn because I'm a grade A fool? I owe it to myself to shut any feelings down I have for my new husband because it's obvious he has none for me, anyway.

CHAPTER 29

TOBIAS

I know she's right, but it hurts just the same. Things were moving too fast, and she has rightly applied the brakes.

Why am I such a fucking bastard? If she knew my past, she would run for cover like Carlos obviously has, because the bastard just won't let me kill him.

My mood has now changed and I need to get my head back in business, so I leave Anastasia to shower and deal with what just happened and head off to find Matteo.

I find him working in the office building to the rear of the house and note the surprise in his eyes as I head inside. "Mr. Moretti."

He nods and stands, and I say irritably. "We're leaving. Arrange it."

"Consider it done."

"Any word on Carlos?"

His eyes light up and I sense a change in him, which immediately gets my attention. "I just had word that he may be in Chicago. I'm having it checked out now and should hear by the end of the day."

"Who's on it?"

"Salvatore."

My fists ball, and I feel the murderous rage taking hold of my reasoning. "Call him, find out what he knows, and arrange our journey home. Then I want you to arrange a trip to Chicago. We leave as soon as we touch down and offload Mrs. Moretti."

He nods and I leave him to the arrangements and growl inside. Carlos Toledo. The little sniveling piece of shit who is the last man standing. I know it was him who brought my world to an end and it will be my greatest pleasure to end his. I need to return and take care of the final piece of the puzzle of my past, and I'm impatient to deal with it.

I head back to my suite and see Anastasia brushing her freshly showered hair and snap, "We're leaving."

I don't even look at her because I can't deal with what is surely on her face right now. She probably hates me and thinks this is something to do with what just happened. It's not. I will deal with that when Carlos is dead and six feet under, because that's all I can think of right now.

The journey home is very different from the one we took before. I am cold, distant and plotting the blackest revenge. Anastasia is withdrawn and keeps her tongue well-hidden, which I'm grateful for and we don't speak, which is in direct contrast to how things were before.

She closes her eyes on the plane, but I know she's not sleeping. She is tight, tense, and is in the process of building a wall around her that keeps me out. It bothers me—a lot, but I don't have time to let it get to me. I'll deal with that later because the only thing on my mind right now is Carlos Toledo.

As soon as we touch down, I turn to her and say in an emotionless voice, "You will travel the last part on your own."

She looks at me in shock as the doors open and the steps

are brought to the aircraft. Outside are three cars, as usual, containing my reserve guards that don't travel with me. She gasps, "You're not coming home."

I push aside the pain I feel when she looks at me with hurt in those gorgeous blue eyes and say firmly, "No, I have business to attend to. Salvatore will make sure you arrive safely back at the house. Sophia will keep you company for however long it takes. There will be no visitors, no phone calls and no leaving the premises even to visit the garden. Do I make myself clear?"

"But?"

Leaning in, I hiss, "Do I make myself clear—answer me?"

She lowers her eyes. "Yes."

"Then go."

I give her a gentle push and she shrugs off my hand and heads outside the aircraft without looking back, and I hate the feeling inside me as she leaves. It's as if someone is ripping a band aid off my most tender part and it burns.

Then the door closes and I watch her safely settled in the middle car and as they ease away, I feel like roaring with frustration and anger. Why now, why her, and why the fuck am I such a fucking bastard?

CHAPTER 30

ANASTASIA

I can't even cry. I sit like a statue in the back of another black car and grieve for the one moment I actually loved. Then it was cruelly taken away, leaving me with nothing left to live for. This is it. My life. A prized possession of Satan himself. He has shown me in one hand the pleasure that two people in love can share and then ripped it away with no antiseptic to take the burn away.

Now I'm to remain a prisoner in his home along with his sister until he decides it's ok. Well, maybe now is the time to make a stand, so I knock on the glass partition and as it slides down, say to the man beside the driver.

"I want to go to my mother's home."

He shakes his head.

"I'm sorry, Mrs. Moretti, but no can do. Mr. Moretti was very specific that you are to remain on lockdown at the mansion."

"But?"

The partition slides back up and I feel the frustration growing. What the fuck? I don't even get a say in my own life anymore.

I feel so angry I could rip the leather off the seats with my bare hands as I suddenly hate Tobias Moretti with a passion. Love and hate are so mixed up right now, and hate appears to be winning the battle.

As we sweep through the large electric gates, I hear them close behind me and feel trapped. I have gone from feeling so free and happy to chained and despairing.

As soon as the door opens, I smack away the hand offered to me and head inside angrily. Bloody bastard. I should have known it was all too good to be true.

I slam the door behind me and Mrs. Billings comes running and by the look in her eye, my anger is not uncommon in this house, and she nods respectfully. "Welcome home, Mrs. Moretti. Would you like me to fetch you anything?"

"Good afternoon, Mrs. Billings, please can you arrange a decanter of whiskey to be delivered to the blue room with one glass?"

She raises her eyes and then I hear a soft laugh coming from the entrance to the West wing.

Looking up, I see Sophia standing watching me, shaking her head. "It figures."

"What?" I stare at her irritably as she shares a look with Mrs. Billings and says gently, "Change that order to two coffees with whiskey chasers and have it delivered to my room."

Then she turns to me and says softly, "We need to have a chat."

Mrs. Billings heads off and I am curious, so follow Sophia toward her own suite of rooms. The decoration in this wing is completely different from the rest of the house. She appears to like modern things and her space is minimalist with a style that wouldn't look out of place in a magazine spread. It's light, airy and uncomplicated, and the only color is provided by the tasteful canvases on the walls and the lamps that are resting on chrome and glass tables. Deep pile scatter rugs provide warmth to a large loft space, and I stare around in amazement as I learn a little more about my sister-in-law.

She points to a large, white leather sofa and says sweetly, "Please sit and make yourself at home. I hope you don't mind me interfering, but I recognized myself in you and know just how you're feeling right now."

She leans forward as she sits with her legs tucked up beside her and grins. "My brother is the biggest asshole that ever lived and I am so done with his moods."

Despite myself, I laugh softly. "He is."

We hear movement and see Mrs. Billings carrying a tray of coffee with a couple of glasses of whiskey and Sophia smiles her thanks. "We will be down for dinner, Mrs. Billings, and will take it in the drawing room."

Mrs. Billings nods, and Sophia hands me a cup of hot coffee.

"Drink this and I'll tell you a story."

"A story?"

I look at her in surprise, and she shrugs. "It doesn't have a happy ending I'm afraid but life is shit, as you are about to discover, or maybe you have already."

Leaning back, I nod because I can't argue with her about that.

She sips her coffee and says sadly, "My brother is the way he is for a very good reason. Rewind six years and things were very different. He was at university studying business like any normal student."

She laughs. "Well, as normal as it gets in our family, anyway."

Suddenly, I'm interested because I'm about to discover their family secret, which can only be a good thing, surely.

She smiles as she thinks back on happier times. "We never had a normal upbringing. My father was in the position Tobias is now. He ruled a crime family with fear and a heart filled with nothing but revenge and consequence. We were kept out of the family business as much as possible and mom tried to raise us to be respectful but never kind."

Her eyes dim and she shrugs. "I know why we had to build a hard shell around our heart because my family has many enemies and we could never show weakness. Tobias escaped as much as he could and wanted to go more into the legitimate side of our family business. Our other brother, Thomas, was the one who thrived on the other side."

"You have a brother?"

I stare at her in surprise, and the tears that form in her eyes tell me this is not a happy memory.

"*Had* a brother. They were twins. Tobias and Thomas, can you imagine two of them? It was hard being the younger sister to two bastards, but I managed to cope."

She makes a joke, at least I think it is, but the bitterness in her eyes tells me her life has been a hard one.

"It all started when I fell in love."

I stare at her sharply, and she shakes her head sadly. "Yes, I dared to think I could lead a normal life. The trouble is, it was doomed from the start because the man I fell in love with was Carlos Toledo. You see, Ana, Carlos was the son of a rival to Don Moretti. He had quite an organization, and they were always fighting for their territory. You know the kind of thing, murder, espionage, drugs and kidnap, usual stuff that goes on under the radar."

I reach for my whiskey chaser because I feel in need of some courage to face her past, and she laughs softly. "Typical Romeo and Juliet, or so I thought. We made plans to run away together because if our families discovered our secret, it would result in a full-blown war. You may ask yourself why I would place him above my family, but you see love does strange things to a young girl's mind, and I didn't see what all the fuss was about. So, with the impetuousness of youth, I packed a bag and snuck out one night. I may live in a fortress but there are no barriers to intention and I had my ways. Carlos was waiting for me and we drove to a motel out of town. You can imagine what happened next because it was all I could think of. I wanted him so badly and as it happens, it wasn't worth the trouble."

She laughs as she sees the surprise on my face. "It hurt, honey, and was over before I realized it happened. I told myself it was normal and pushed away my disappointment. I was a woman now—his woman and nothing would ever get in my way. Carlos told me to stay put and he would arrange our escape and I believed him. He was gone for hours, which turned into the next day, and I was so damned worried about him. He never came back, so I called for a cab to take me home because I had nowhere else to go. He didn't return my calls, and I was so afraid he had been discovered and slaughtered by my family. What I didn't expect was that it was the other way around."

I gasp and watch as the tears roll down her face as she sobs, "There were so many guards at the house when I returned. Tobias was summoned and the look in his eye told me something really bad had happened and it wasn't just a result of my escape. He was so angry, Ana. His rage was so great I actually feared for my life. He took my arm and marched me down the hallway toward the stairs to my parent's room. He opened the door, and I saw a nightmare. There was blood everywhere, on the walls, on the bed, and on the carpet. I started to scream, and he pulled me downstairs to my father's den, where the same scene swam before my eyes. Then he shook me like a madman and told me it was all my fault. Our parents were dead because of the company I kept. Thomas was out on a killing spree to revenge our parent's execution and the person responsible for setting it all up was Carlos Toledo."

She is broken. I can see that for myself as she sobs with her head in her hands as the full horrors of her past come back to this room.

I head over and pull her in my arms and stroke her hair because it's the only comfort I can give her. I'm not sure what to say because her story is a true horror one and I can't imagine the grief something like that brings.

After a while, she settles back and sniffs. "Thomas never came back. Not alive, anyway. His body was delivered to our front gate, cut into pieces in a trash bag. There were many casualties on both sides and for a while everyone retreated to count their troops. We had lost our parents and our much-loved brother, and all of this fell on Tobias's unwilling shoulders. It destroyed him. He became hard and cold and prone to violent rages. He had lost a vital part of him when Thomas died, and he vowed he would never again let himself feel the loss of a loved one. Maybe now you can understand why he keeps his heart so well guarded. It brought him to his knees and revenge was the only antidote to a lifetime of pain."

It all slots into place and my heart aches for my husband. I understand now and know he had to distance himself from me, not because he wanted to, but because he needed to.

I feel like such a fool—again and wish he was here so I could tell him it doesn't matter. I can live without love as long as I live my life with him.

The tears fall from my own eyes as I picture the past this family has lived through and then Sophia says, "Tobias ended the war."

"How?"

Her face tells me I'm not going to like what I hear next, and she has a wild, feral look about her as she hisses. "He hunted every one of the Toledo family down and their men and slaughtered them personally."

I feel sick and wish she hadn't told me. Tobias murdered not one but many people, and I feel sick.

"It's where they are now, looking for Carlos."

I stare at her in shock and she says bitterly, "He escaped every time. No matter where he was seen, he was always somewhere else when they went looking. He used me to find information about my family that he wanted to use to kill them all and make his family more powerful. He took my virginity as an bonus, not because he loved me, but because he could. I will never forgive him and hope Tobias does find him and tortures him long and hard because the torture we were left with on a daily basis is hard to live with."

"But how can he murder people and get away with it?"

Sophia stares at me incredulously and laughs. "He is a master at covering his tracks. None of this leads back to this door. The cops may think they know, but they know shit. Tobias is too clever to get caught. You see, Ana, we have trained for this our whole life. It's what we do. Hide behind respectability with an undercurrent of menace that keeps the questions from our door."

Suddenly, her cell phone rings and she looks down and says in a dull voice, "It's Tobias, I should take this."

As I watch her expression change from resignation to fear, I feel a prickle of danger heading my way. She just says, "I'm on it."

As she cuts the call, she turns to me and her eyes are wide and frightened as she whispers, "We have to leave."

CHAPTER 31

TOBIAS

As soon as we touched down in Chicago, the cars were waiting. Matteo briefed me on the way. Carlos has been sighted around the district and a reliable source wired the mansion yesterday with the news. Michael D'Angelo runs the biggest crime family here, and so we head straight for his offices downtown.

Matteo called ahead and informed him we were coming and, as we skid to a halt outside his tower block, my men accompany me inside.

They are asked to wait in reception and only Matteo and I are granted access to speak with the man himself and I am anxious that we don't miss our chance to finally get our hands on my most wanted.

We are shown to his office and as the man who walks the same path as me stands, the look on his face is of mild curiosity.

"Tobias, to what do I owe this pleasure?"

Matteo stiffens beside me and I say darkly, "You tell me, Michael. We had word from you that Carlos was in town."

From the look on his face, I know we've been played and I

feel the blood scorching my soul as he shakes his head. "Not from me, Tobias, I would have called you personally."

Matteo immediately reaches for his cell and calls the mansion, and I can hear someone talking rapidly on the other end.

Michael looks concerned. "Anything we can help you with?"

Feeling like a fool, I say angrily, "I'm sorry to have bothered you. It appears our information was misdirected."

I turn to leave, and Michael says no more. He knows I've been played, it's obvious, and like fools we raced here without checking the facts first, just to get our hands on the one man that escapes me.

As we walk, I snap, "What the fuck, Matteo, who the hell is responsible for this?"

"I'm on it, sir. Our instructions came from Harlow. He is loyal throughout, so I trusted him."

"Maybe that was your first mistake."

He falls silent as I grab my cell and dial Sophia's number, hoping she answers. As I hear her voice, I snap, "Take Ana and leave. You're not safe. Carlos may be in the area and will come for you there. I'm not sure who we can trust because someone there is playing us. Matteo will arrange transport and make sure you keep your head down and your wits about you."

I cut the call, feeling so helpless I want to kill someone. We are miles away in the wrong bloody state and it will take us hours to return, hours we don't have and a traitor in our midst.

Matteo speaks urgently on the phone and, as he cuts the call, says in a low voice, "I called for Vincenzo. He will collect your family and take them to Ana's sister. She has contacts that are above the law and will provide a safe refuge."

My heart twists as I know just where they're heading.

Twisted Reaper MC. Fucking bikers who hide their real role behind their steel-clad walls. Government assassins who, as Matteo said, are completely above the law. As much as I hate the thought of either of them in that fuck palace, even I agree it's the safest place for them.

Turning to Matteo, I snap, "Cancel Vincenzo. I want Angel to collect them. She's the only one I trust."

Matteo nods and dials Ana's sister and I hope to God she can pull this off because if Carlos gets his hands on the two most important people to me in the world, I am fucked.

ANASTASIA

Sophia turns to me and says in a whisper. "Tobias thinks that Carlos may be in town heading our way. He is arranging a car to collect us and take us somewhere safe. We can't trust anyone, so follow my lead and I'll do my darnedest to keep us from being killed."

The fear in my heart is now very real as I nod and follow her to the top of the stairs leading down.

She listens and then sets her shoulders back and hisses, "Act natural."

As we reach the foot of the stairs, there is silence around us and she says quickly, "Follow me outside."

As we make to leave, Angelo heads out and says apologetically, "I'm sorry. You cannot leave the house."

Sophia rolls her eyes and heads toward him, swaying her hips suggestively. "Listen, Angelo, you may have your loyalty to my brother, but you're on my staff now. I command you to let us go."

He stands firm and looks so unhappy I feel sorry for him as he shakes his head. "I'm sorry, I have my instructions."

Then I watch in disbelief as Sophia heads closer and with one lift of her arm, presses her hand against his neck and he falls to the ground out cold. "Pressure points, you've gotta love them. Shame really, I liked having him around."

"Is he…?"

"No, just out cold, but we don't have long. Come on."

She wrenches open the door and as she does, a black car is waiting and she smiles. "This must be the one Tobias arranged."

She heads over to the car and opens the door and then, to my horror, she is pulled roughly inside and the door slams and the car pulls away at speed. "Sophia!"

I scream after her and suddenly the guards are pouring out from every doorway. "What happened?"

One of them looks after the car, as several of the men jump into nearby cars and tear after it. "Sophia was forced into that car; I think it may be Carlos."

The man lifts his cell and I can hear him issuing instructions and I stare around me in amazement at the scene before me. There is shouting and doors slamming and the squeak of tires as they give chase and then the man beside me says urgently, "Come with me."

"No, I can't. I must stay here. Tobias said so."

Before I know what's happening, he hauls me over his shoulder and carries me toward the gates and I scream, struggling to get away. "Shut the fuck up, I'm saving your life."

"What?"

As we reach the gates, I see another car heading toward us and as it stops, someone jumps out and shouts, "Ana, it's ok, you're safe."

Angel runs toward me and says to the guard, "Thank you, she'll be ok."

He drops me and I run toward her with the tears running

just as fast and sob as she pushes me into the car and before I know it, we are tearing off at speed.

I think I'm in shock as she says softly, "It's ok, honey, you're safe now."

"But Sophia."

I can't even imagine what her fate is, and Angel shakes her head. "I'm sorry, honey. I don't know what happened. We received a call from someone called Matteo, who told us that you were in danger and to come and get you. We must take you to the Reapers where you'll be safe."

"The Reapers, you mean…"

"Yes, the guys I trust with my life. You won't come to any harm there, honey, and I'll wait with you until this is resolved."

"What if it isn't?" I stare at her fearfully, and she shakes her head sadly. "Then we will deal with what that means when and if it happens."

I notice that Sebastian is driving, and he says softly, "I'm sorry, Anastasia, you must be wondering what the hell is happening."

"You could say that."

I can't think about anything than Sophia being pulled into a car and I fear what could happen to her if Carlos was the one inside. Tobias would never recover if his sister arrived home the same way as his brother, and my heart breaks for him. It's all too much and I place my head in my hands and cry so hard I barely register the comforting arm my sister puts around me.

Then, as the minutes turn to hours on our journey, I fall into a fitful sleep.

CHAPTER 32

TOBIAS

By the time we touch down, I am so angry I almost can't speak. Matteo told me what happened at the house, and the only thing that settles me is that Ana is with Angel and Sebastian. If they reach the Twisted Reaper MC, they will be safe and I snap, "Any update on my wife?"

Matteo consults his phone and nods. "They checked in twenty minutes ago. They are an hour away from the Rubicon."

"And my sister?"

He shakes his head. "The cars lost them somewhere outside of Jackson County. We have a trace on Sophia's cell, but when we located it, it was in a ditch off the highway. It appears it was tossed from the window. We have men out combing the area and our guy tracing the vehicle registration, but so far, it's come up as unknown.

I make a fist and hate the feeling of helplessness that consumes me and I snap, "Have you found out who the traitor is?"

Matteo nods, and his expression tells me I'm not gonna like it.

"It's Todd."

"Todd!" I stare at him in total surprise, because Todd has always been one of my most loyal guards. He was with my father before me and was almost one of the family. "Has he confessed?"

Matteo nods. "He broke down when questioned by your enforcers."

Luckily, I have a team of men who are my enforcers, men that have no soul and carry out the shadier side of the business. My own band of assassins who love to invoke terror and fear in the men I instruct them to find. I called them from Chicago and asked them to flush out the traitor, and as usual they have done so with ease.

"Where is he?"

"In the holding cell."

"Take me there."

The cars are waiting and we waste no time in heading toward the holding cell, which is approximately twenty minutes away. It's a deserted farm I use on the edge of town that is private and secure. I take my business there that I want to hide, and Todd is now my main concern.

Throughout the journey, I hear Matteo getting updates and still nothing. My anger knows no bounds as I think of ways to extract the information I need from the man who has betrayed me after generations spent in my organization.

∼

We are soon at the holding cell and I waste no time in heading straight inside, reaching for the sharpest knife from the rack as I pass.

I see him bound and gagged in a chair on the concrete floor, and his eyes look at me with fear and resignation. He knows what's coming.

Nodding to one of my enforcers, he rips the gag from Todd's mouth and he gasps for air, looking so wretched I spit on the ground.

He says in a rough voice, "It's not what you think."

"What do I think, Todd?"

My voice is low and menacing, and he starts to shake.

"I didn't betray you. I took the call, that's all. I thought it was D'Angelo, I had every reason to believe it was him. I would never betray you."

Matteo shakes his head and whispers in my ear and I snap, "Then how do you explain the thousands of dollars that were deposited in your bank just 24 hours ago?"

Todd looks down. "I can't."

"And how do you explain the tickets booked in your name to Rome, along with the rest of your family—one way?"

"It wasn't me."

I stride across and hit him hard across the face, and his head rolls back and blood spurts from his nose.

Holding the knife to his throat, I relish the fear in his eyes as I growl, "Where is he; where has he taken my sister?"

He starts to shake as I lay the blade against his throat and says fearfully, "I don't know."

Taking one of his hands, I lay it out on the arm of the wooden seat and hold the knife to his finger. "I will cut these off one at a time until you tell me what I want to hear."

The tears roll down his face as he stutters, "He'll kill them. He has my wife and kids."

"Talk to me."

He starts to cry, and I look at him in disgust. "A few days back, he sent me a video of them tied up in a steel cell. He told me if I fed you just one piece of false information, they would be spared and waiting for me on the flight to Rome. He would pay me well for my trouble and we would be safe with his organization in Italy. If you found out, he would kill them all. I had to do it, Mr. Moretti, they're family."

I squeeze my eyes tightly shut and feel the rage flooding through me. "Your family, what about mine? My sister could be dead because you didn't come to me first. You should have known we would deal with him. Family is everything, Todd and you placed yours above mine and that was your first mistake."

I snap to Matteo. "Find his phone. I need to see the picture and analyze it because if he's got Todd's family, it may be where he's taken Sophia. Send it to my phone."

Matteo heads across the room and lifts Todd's jacket from the floor, and I watch him scroll through the cell. Then I hear my phone ping and as I look at the photograph, I see why Todd was so worried. His wife is tied up with her hands above her to a ring on the wall. His two kids are beside her and appear to have been drugged. She is naked, and it looks as if she's taken quite a beating and I feel sick. What would I have done if I saw Ana or Sophia like this? I expect anything I could to keep them safe. Yet he betrayed me.

He is starting to sob and I hate the weakness in him and turn away, snapping, "Keep him here and for fuck's sake gag the bastard."

Then I do something I don't normally do and type a message and press send. I need help on this and know just who to ask because they have more intel than the president. The very people who I sent my most valuable possession to and the only ones I can trust.

Then I walk away from Todd and back to the car, with Matteo close behind. "Take me back to the mansion, we need to wait for instructions."

I tell him nothing because I am keeping this close. If anyone can save my sister, they can, and I just hope it's not too late.

CHAPTER 33

ANASTASIA

I wake and it's dark outside and we are on a rough track. Angel says softly, "We're here, Ana, my second home."

I look out of the window but can't see anything, just heavily dense forest and no sign of life.

"What here, in the forest?"

She nods, and I can tell she's excited. I feel curious as to where she went for the five years she was gone and I'm about to find out.

As we reach the end of the bumpy track, I see a large courtyard clearing where a huge structure dominates the skyline. It's so dark out here, yet as soon as we approach, a searchlight picks up our car and illuminates a steel-clad building standing proudly in the forest.

Angel seems excited and says, "I can't wait for you to meet my second family."

Sebastian throws me a pitying look, and I wonder what that means. Surely, they can't be that bad because Angel wouldn't bring me somewhere that wasn't safe.

Then I think of Sophia, and my heart pounds. God, I hope

she's somewhere safe by now. I hope the guards chased them down and rescued her. I can't begin to imagine the pain Tobias will go through if she isn't.

As we step outside, Angel looks around and seems distracted.

Then she turns to Sebastian and says in a worried voice, "Half the bikes are missing."

I stare at her in surprise because I've never seen so many bikes in one place before, and Sebastian shrugs. "Maybe they're on a job and will back later."

I fall silent because I cannot begin to understand what they are talking about, and as we approach the huge wooden door, I read the sign above it.

'Abandon hope all who enter here.'

Angel laughs as she sees the expression on my face. "Don't worry, honey, it's just there to scare the traders away."

She winks, but I don't believe her for a second.

She enters some kind of code in a security panel and the door swings open and we head inside.

The first thing we see is a huge guy bearing down on us. He is so ferocious looking; I hide behind Sebastian as Angel squeals and runs straight into his arms. "Brewer, I've missed you."

"Hey, honey, I thought it might be you."

"Why?"

"Because we had word you were coming."

"Tobias." He nods.

At the sound of my husband's name, I peer out and see the guy looking at me with interest. He appears slightly older, but that doesn't stop him from looking pumped and ready to cut a man down on the spot.

Angel takes my hand and says proudly, "Meet my sister, Anastasia. This is Brewer, a real good friend of mine."

He nods and then says good naturedly, "You look like sisters. God help us, two Angels in this place, we can't cope."

He winks as Angel rolls her eyes. As we follow him down a long passageway, she asks, "Where are the rest of the guys?"

"On a job."

"That's unlike you not to go with them."

He shrugs. "Said I'd stay behind to keep the home fires burning."

Angel shares a look with him, and for some reason I think it concerns me. Then she says softly, "When will they be back?"

"Not sure, they're out of state."

She can't question him further because he opens a door and we find ourselves in a huge room that appears to be a bar. There is loud music blaring from speakers and I can see huge television sets placed on walls around the room, where more guys like him sit on couches with attractive girls in one hand and a beer in another.

There's a huge cheer as Angel walks in, and I watch in disbelief as she squeals and runs around hugging everyone. I look at Sebastian in surprise and he shrugs but I can tell he's not happy, as one by one, the scariest guys I have ever seen, hug and kiss her as if she's a long-lost girlfriend.

Then it hits me. She probably is and, in a flash, I see just how she's been living for the past five years. Here, among these people, and it's no wonder she's hardened up so much.

I feel a little awkward until a pretty girl comes across and says sweetly, "Oh my god, you must be Angel's sister, Anastasia, isn't it?"

I nod shyly and she hugs me to my surprise and says, "I'm

Millie, Angel's best friend here. She's told me so much about you, but I'm afraid not all of it was good."

She winks and looks at Sebastian, and I roll my eyes. "I'm sure she had quite a few things to say about me but it's good now."

Angel comes across and I watch as they hug it out and feel a little tinge of jealously toward my older sister. It's obvious these people love her very much and the same for her, and it appears that she found much more of a home here than the one we shared.

Sebastian looks like a duck out of water until Brewer says good naturedly, "Come on, man, I'll get you a beer. You must be shot to pieces after that journey."

Sebastian follows him and Angel whispers to Millie, "Do you know where the guys have gone?"

"Not sure but they won't be back tonight, more's the pity."

She catches me looking and smiles. "Girl, this place is a candy store. Look around you, these guys are seriously hot and largely available. The ones that ain't are like brothers, so it's all good. Anyway, let's get you both a drink before you hit the hay. We have a lot to catch up on."

Feeling a little self-conscious, I follow them to the bar and Millie jumps over it and laughs. "I'm guessin' a white wine each, am I right?"

We both nod and she starts pouring the drinks. Then I see Angel's eyes light up as a pretty redhead heads our way. "Bonnie, come over and meet my sister."

Bonnie heads over and I can't help but like the pretty girl on sight. Angel says happily, "Bonnie is one of the old ladies here."

Bonnie laughs at my expression and winks. "Not so old, in appearance, anyway. Inside I'm 103 courtesy of my old man."

They laugh and Angel says proudly, "That old man is the

second commander-in-chief here next to Ryder King. Where is he, by the way?"

Bonnie looks at me and says kindly. "They went out of state. They had a call from your sister's husband concerning his sister and they located them."

I stare at her in shock and stutter, "Oh, please god, have they found her?"

Bonnie nods. "Last I heard, they had the premises surrounded and were about to go in. Don't worry, honey, they are the best and your sister-in-law is in safe hands if…"

She breaks off and I see the concern in her eyes as I finish her sentence for her. "Alive."

Angel looks concerned, and I slump back in my seat, the tears threatening to spill. Poor Sophia, she's been through so much already.

Bonnie lays her hand on my arm and says softly, "I'm sure she'll be fine. They located her quickly, so she may have a chance."

"When will you know?"

"Soon, I hope. Brewer stayed to coordinate the intel, and Ryder took Snake and eight others with him. They took the plane so may be back later but it's late, so they may stay at the Dragon's Ruin."

"The what?"

Angel whispers, "Local biker gang's clubhouse. They work together across the states and the Reapers use the local MC clubs when they need back up."

I fall silent because this is a world I know little about and yet being here, in the thick of madness, it doesn't feel so strange anymore. Then my thoughts turn to Tobias and I say fearfully, "What about my husband, is he there?"

Bonnie shakes her head. "We're expecting him soon."

"What here?" I stare at her in alarm, and she nods. "As

soon as they got the call, Ryder told him to come. They will finish their business here at the Rubicon."

Angel looks worried, and I feel my heart beating faster. Tobias is coming here, this is really happening, shit is about to get real, and I can only sit back and watch the fireworks.

CHAPTER 34

TOBIAS

As soon as I got the call from the Reapers, I instructed Matteo to round up ten of my men and take us to the airport. We could be in Washington in one hour by plane and unlike Ana, who would have taken several hours to get there, we will be there by the time the Reapers return.

I haven't decided what to do with Todd. He can sweat it out until the dust settles and as we drive to the airfield, Matteo says in his usual calm voice, "What's the plan?"

"I sent the information you gave me to Ryder King."

Matteo looks worried, and I shrug. "I had no choice. I needed action, and fast. He has the technology to trace any vehicle and go in and rescue, so I trust him to do the right thing."

Matteo nods and I say darkly, "They didn't take long to trace it. The license plate was false but on their radar, and it linked to another plate they had intel on. It was reported as stolen, but the vehicle was fitted with a tracking device. They used Sophia's phone signal to locate the area it was seen last and then latched onto the tracker by satellite. It was found at an abandoned remote cement works out of town, and they called the local MC club to take a look. Meanwhile, they made their way to the scene ready to storm the building and I just hope they're not too late."

Matteo whistles loudly. "Man, that's some operation they got there. Won't it cause you problems, don't they work for the government?"

"They did me a favor, no questions asked. When they found out it was Angel's sister-in-law, they couldn't move fast enough. What you also have to understand is these guys deal with the trash for the government and no one deserves that title more than Carlos Toledo. If he went on trial, he would be out in a few years and he is not worth the red tape. If they hand him to me, it's my shit to shovel, so everyone's happy."

"Everyone except Carlos."

Matteo laughs softly and I snap, "Save your laughter for when we've dealt with the scum. He may have the last laugh, after all, he still has Sophia."

We soon reach the plane and as I settle in my seat, I feel the nerves mingling with a thirst for revenge. God help Carlos if Sophia is harmed in any way. I can't lose her, she's all I have left and now I know Ana is safe, my full attention is on saving my sister.

The plane is soon eating up the distance and I'm intolerable company, so the guys leave me to brood about things on my own.

As soon as the plane stops and the door opens, I am almost running down the stairs because I can't get to Ana quickly enough. Just to feel her safe in my arms is the only thing I want, and that will give me the power to deal with what comes next.

As usual, the cars are waiting, and we head off to the Rubicon, the home of the Twisted Reaper MC.

On the journey, I check constantly for an update and the

radio silence is killing me inside. I've never been one for patience, and feeling so helpless is tearing my heart out.

I know the guys will be uncomfortable going to the home of paid assassins, but I had no choice. This time I would do anything to save my family, and there is only one loose cannon left in a war that should have been over years ago.

As soon as we reach the yard, I look out and see several men lined up in front of the steel-clad building, and Matteo whistles. "Will you look at that?"

I expected a welcoming committee, but these guys are hard-assed bastards who are the most part ex-navy SEALS. They will be wary of us because my reputation is a bad one and entertaining the mafia is not something they do on a regular basis.

My door opens and I step outside and one of the guys steps forward and holds out his hand. "Mr. Moretti, I'm Brewer, Ryder told us to expect you."

I shake his hand and say quickly, "My wife?"

"Inside, she's safe with her sister."

"Can I see her?"

"Of course. Your men can stay in the accommodation we have out back."

He turns and shouts to the men behind him. "Chase, Jet, show the men where to go."

Two guys step forward and the rest just stare with interest. I detect no animosity and my men are under strict instructions to behave, so I follow Brewer into the building, with Matteo by my side.

As we walk, I say, "Any news?"

"None, they're on radio silence. It could be a while."

I fall silent because that was not what I wanted to hear. This is pure torture waiting for someone else to do a job I should be in charge of and I just have to suck it up and trust the professionals who do this kind of thing all the time.

Brewer opens the door to a large bar area and I scan the room desperately in search of Ana. It makes me shiver to see the type of place this is, and I feel the eyes on me from every corner of the room. Then I see her and as our eyes meet, she is up and running. I can't get to her quickly enough and as she falls into my arms, I lock her in the tightest embrace and feel the relief hit me hard. She's with me where she belongs.

I bury my face in her hair and inhale the scent of everything I hold dear and she whispers, "I'm so sorry, Tobias."

"For what?"

"For acting like a child. It doesn't matter if you can't love me, I will love us both doubly hard to make up for it."

Her words twist my heart and for a moment, I have no words. This woman, this innocent, sweet woman, is so much better than me and she doesn't even realize it.

Somebody coughs nearby and I look up and see Brewer nod toward the door. Immediately, I pull back and stare at my beautiful wife and whisper, "Don't go anywhere, we need to talk but business first."

I note the worry in her eyes and share it. She knows what's at stake, I can tell, and so I lean down and kiss her lips softly and whisper, "Just for the record, I do love you."

Then I leave and don't look back. I can only guess her expression and it makes me feel good that I got to tell her what I haven't admitted to myself. I do love Anastasia Johnson, and this last twenty-four hours has reinforced that fact. Somehow love has found a way into the blackest heart and far from feeling worried, I can't wait to see what that means.

CHAPTER 35

ANASTASIA

Tobias said he loves me. I can't believe it. My hand flies to my mouth where his just left and I stare after him in total shock. Then the tears build as I realize what he just gave me. It must have taken so much for him to say those words, especially when he is so worried about his sister.

Angel comes up behind me and places a hand on my shoulder. "Is everything ok, Ana?"

I nod. "Yes, I think it is."

I follow Angel back to the bar and wonder what's happening outside. Tobias looked so worried, and I share it. Sophia told me the type of man they are dealing with and I can't shake the feeling something bad is going to happen.

I think we wait for close on two hours before the bar starts to empty and Millie yawns. "I'm heading to bed, alone unfortunately."

She pulls a face and Angel laughs. "Never mind, honey, tomorrow's another day."

She turns to Sebastian and says softly, "What about you, honey, do you want to grab some sleep?"

He shakes his head and the look he shoots her makes me smile. They always have loved each other unconditionally and nobody knows that more than me.

"No, I'll stay with you."

She shakes her head. "I'll be fine and just curl up here with Ana."

Something in her expression makes him change his mind, and he nods. "Ok, but call me the minute something happens."

I watch them kiss softly, and my heart lifts. They made it through, which is good to see. Maybe I did too. If today turns out for the best, I will feel happy again. But I can't think of that all the time Sophia is out there with a madman.

Soon we are alone in the bar and Angel says gently, "Come and sit with me. We can wait here, so we're on hand if news comes in."

I nod and sit beside her, and she grabs a nearby blanket and covers us both. "This is like old times, honey."

I nod. "That seems a long time ago."

"I wonder what we would have thought if we knew how our lives would turn out. Me an MC whore before finding true love with my childhood sweetheart and you married to the mob."

We both giggle and I say in a whisper, "Tobias just told me he loved me."

Angel's eyes widen and she gasps, "No way, you mean he has a heart."

"It appears so."

"So, tell me about your honeymoon, the boat, the island. What was it like? Actually, scrub that, what was *he* like?"

She winks and I say wistfully. "It was so good, Angel. I never really thought it would be, but he was so kind, caring, and considerate. He made me feel like a queen and then it changed."

"What do you mean—changed?"

Her eyes narrow and I shrug. "He withdrew from me because I told him I loved him."

Reaching out, Angel takes my hand. "Oh honey, that must have hurt."

"It did. Immediately, he arranged for us to go home and we didn't speak all the way. Then he kicked me out of the plane and left me to go home alone in one of his cars. I felt so bad, I thought he didn't want me anymore."

Angel looks angry on my behalf, and I say in a worried voice. "Then Sophia told me all about what happened when their parents died. It was brutal, Angel, it's no wonder Tobias withdrew. His heart was broken, and he became consumed with the thirst for revenge. He told me he could never allow himself to love again, and it was because Carlos Toledo arranged the murder of his entire family. Now he's got Sophia and I'm so afraid. He's a man with no soul and won't care what he does to her. Poor Tobias, he could lose the one person he's got left. His parents and twin were brutally murdered, and he went to hell and back. In fact, I think he's still there because Carlos is still out there."

Angel's face mirrors my concern, and she squeezes my hand reassuringly. "It's ok, honey. The Reapers know what they're doing. They are the best and if Sophia's alive, they will bring her safely back."

"That's what I'm afraid of. What if she's dead? It will destroy Tobias; he may not recover."

We fall silent and as the clock ticks on the wall, I feel his pain and pray to God that Sophia makes it.

∽

WE MUST FALL asleep because I hear voices in the distance and jerk awake, unsure for a moment where I am. Angel stirs and blinks, before looking at me with fear in her eyes. "They're back."

Quickly, we jump up and head for the door because, by the sounds of it, there are quite a number of people out there and as I glance at the clock, I can see it's 7 am.

Angel opens the door and I see several huge men heading wearily inside and she says fearfully, "Is she ok?"

One of the guys sees her and smiles. "Well, if it isn't our little Angel."

He looks at me with interest and Angel snaps, "For fuck's sake, Tyson, is she safe?"

He nods, and the relief is overwhelming, and I lean against the wall for support.

He adds, "She's with Ryder and Snake. They took her to the office where her brother is. Hang tight, I'm sure they won't be long."

Angel turns and her smile says it all. Sophia's safe, thank God.

CHAPTER 36

TOBIAS

We got news in the early hours they had Sophia. They were taking her to the Dragon's ruin to get cleaned up, and that sent me out of my mind. Cleaned up, what the hell happened?

I sat for three torturous hours as we waited, and Brewer filled me in and kept the coffee coming. They went in when they had eyes on Carlos. Sophia was chained to a wall next to Todd's wife, and the kids were slumped on the ground. Carlos was shouting and brandishing a knife and shouting that he was gonna kill them all. Apparently, the Reapers went in covertly and had the element of surprise on their side. Carlos was ambushed and knocked senseless, and the prisoners were freed by the guys. Snake cut Sophia free and got her the hell out of there, and Ryder dealt with Carlos. They warned me he's not a pretty sight because one thing the Reapers hate above everything is when kids are involved. I think they all had their turn and Brewer told me he would probably be out for a while.

Todd's family was taken to the nearest hospital, and Ryder made sure any questions would be buried.

As soon as we hear the commotion, I stand and steel myself for what I will see. Sophia means everything to me, and if I see one blemish on her beautiful face or body, I'm liable to lose any self-control I may have left.

I'm not prepared for what I see though and as they crowd into the room; I see her staring at me with a pale face, and her eyes are wide and frightened. She looks so frail and nothing like the strong woman she is, and my gut twists in a silent rage. She is broken, it's in her eyes. She has that look of a woman who can't deal with the horror she's faced and as I make toward her, Ryder says softly, "Back off, man."

What the fuck? I look at him sharply and he shakes his head and gently takes her hand and says softly, "It's ok, darlin', your brother's here. You're safe now, and no one here is gonna hurt you. Now, I want you to take that seat and I'll get you some hot tea, is that ok, darlin'?"

She just nods and sits in the seat without looking at me once. Ryder turns to another guy and says in a whisper, "Fetch Bonnie, she'll help her."

I'm not sure what's happening and Ryder nods for me to follow him outside and as the door clicks shut, he says in a low voice. "She's in shock. The bastard roughed her up and put the fear of god in her. She hasn't said much, but she's scared. My advice would be to get her checked out because there's no telling what damage that bastard did."

"Where is he?" My voice is tight and controlled, but my rage isn't.

Ryder nods in understanding. "We've tossed him in the pit. He's out cold and will wake in the ground with no light or way out. He's yours, but he can stay there until you're ready."

I feel impatient to deal with him, but Sophia has to come first.

Before we go back in, I see a sleepy looking redhead come toward us looking concerned and Ryder says, "Bonnie, she's in there, see what you can do."

She nods and heads inside and Ryder says fondly, "Bonnie's good. If anyone can get through to her, she can. I would have sent for my wife, but she's about to go into labor and can do without this."

"And you left her—for me?"

I stare at Ryder in astonishment, and he shrugs. "She told me to go. She's not due for a few more days, and we weren't that far. If I had to, I would have come back."

"Even so, thank you. It means a lot."

One of Ryder's men comes out and says angrily, "Fucking bastard. I didn't hit him hard enough, she's a mess in there."

I make to move past him and he holds up his hand. "Give them a minute. Bonnie's good, she'll sort her out."

We must wait for a good twenty minutes before Bonnie pokes her head around the door and says softly, "We're heading off so Sophia can have a bath and a fresh change of clothes. She's still not talking but has agreed to let me help her."

I feel the fury grip me hard. What the fuck did he do to my sister?

Ryder says firmly, "We will leave them to it. It's best to let her settle in. We'll grab some breakfast and then you can decide what you want to do."

The last thing I feel like doing is eating, but the guys look done in, so I nod and follow them to a large canteen area where one of the guys is cooking up eggs and bacon.

My own men have joined them and we must look a strange bunch. I see Angel and Ana and immediately head across to my wife. Her face is full of concern and she whispers, "How is she?"

"Not good. She's not talking and appears in shock. Someone's with her now."

Ana looks so worried, I reach across and grab her hand. "She's alive, that's all that matters. The rest we can deal with."

We sit for close on two hours before Bonnie heads back and I watch her whisper something urgently to Ryder and his right-hand man. Ryder looks up and I see him nod, and then Bonnie heads off and Ryder comes across. "I'm sorry, man."

"What for?" I feel ice freeze my blood as he sits beside me and says softly, "She won't see you. She told Bonnie she won't go home with you and wants to stay here."

"What the fuck?"

Ana places her hand on my arm and says softly, "Is that the shock talking?"

"Maybe. We will get her checked out by a doctor, but for now I would do as she says. She needs to heal and you must let her."

"What, leave her here? I won't, she belongs with me."

Ryder looks at him sympathetically. "Listen, it's been a shock for everyone, and she's probably not thinking straight. Give her a few days and then we'll see where we're at. Go home and take that trash in the pit with you. I don't want to know what you decide and if anyone asks, I never met the guy."

He stands and I feel helpless as I think of leaving Sophia here. He smiles and shakes his head. "She's not the first broken Angel we've fixed, and she won't be the last. Leave her with us and trust us to do what's best for her."

Angel leans across and says softly, "Listen to Ryder, Tobias. He knows what he's talking about and I know the Reapers. Sophia's in the best place she could be and she will come back to you when she is good and ready."

I can't think straight, but I know I have no choice. She is

fragile. It was obvious to anyone with eyes and so I say with thick emotion, "Can I see her—just to say goodbye?"

"I'm sorry, man." Ryder's voice is sympathetic but firm, and I know that's his last word. I just have to trust he knows what he's doing and nod.

"I'll go. Have my men retrieve Carlos and we'll leave you in peace."

Standing up, I take Ana's hand and pull her to my side where she belongs.

"Come, let's go home."

∽

Leaving my sister behind is the hardest thing I have ever had to do, but Ryder's right. She needs to heal and she can't do that with the memories back at home. Maybe this is the best place for her, only time will tell, but whatever Sophia needs, she gets and this is no exception.

So, after we say our goodbyes and I thank the Reapers from the bottom of my black heart, we leave Angel and Sebastian to drive themselves and head back to the plane and home.

CHAPTER 37

ANASTASIA

Tobias is pre-occupied, and who can blame him? In fact, the whole party is exhausted and I wonder what happened back at the mansion when I left.

We arrived at the airfield and I couldn't wait to get on board and back home. Leaving Sophia was painful, and our natural reaction was to want her with us, but Angel assured us she was in the right place. I'm not sure what the way out of this will be, but all I know is the only person I want by my side is holding my hand so tenderly it makes my heart lift out of the stormiest sea. Whatever happens, I have him and now I know he actually feels something for me; I am happy with that.

We hardly speak on the journey home, which thankfully is a short one. As soon as we touch down, the cars are waiting and I can't wait to get home and grab a change of clothes and some sleep. It's been an emotional few days and I'm tired.

Tobias looks a wreck, which is the first sign since I met him that he's human after all, and when the door to the car closes and we are alone, he sinks his head in his hands and his voice breaks. "I hate leaving her there."

I rub his back and yet have no words. I share his concern.

"It could have been so different. If I hadn't called the Reapers, we would never have found her."

"Where's Carlos?"

"Being unloaded like cargo and taken to a place I own."

I wish I hadn't asked, but know his fate will not be a happy one. Tobias sits up and reaches for me and pulls me close, and I feel his breath fan my face. "You give me strength, little bird. I will see this through for you and for Sophia."

I can feel my heart quicken and know this particular storm isn't over yet. "What will you do?"

I'm not sure I really want to know, but he rests his head against mine and whispers, "I will end this."

Then he kisses me softly and with a desperation that strikes fear in my heart. What is he thinking, it's impossible to tell?

One kiss that feels so loving soon turns into one of passion. He fists my hair in his hand and kisses me long and hard and despite the situation, I feel the desire growing and he says huskily, "Never leave me, Ana, now you're mine I never want to lose what we have."

"I'm going nowhere." I whisper the words and he sighs and I can tell he's going through some powerful emotions right now and my heart aches for him.

The car stops and I see we've reached home and it's like a welcome rainbow after a storm.

As the door opens, Tobias helps me from the car and Matteo nods respectfully. "Welcome home, Mrs. Moretti."

As I look up at the impressive building, my heart settles. Yes, I'm home, because wherever Tobias is, is where I belong.

Mrs. Billings meets us looking anxious, and I smile at her

reassuringly. She must have been scared, and I wonder how much she knows. "Mr. Moretti, Mrs. Moretti, it's good to see you. Can I fetch you anything?"

Tobias turns to me and I say gratefully, "Some coffee would be good, thank you."

Tobias nods and leans down, whispering, "I'll meet you in the kitchen, I need to talk to Matteo first."

He walks off with his right-hand man toward the office wing and I follow Mrs. Billings into the kitchen and feel the relief hit me hard. We made it.

Then I look at the thin woman who deals with so much and say gently, "You must have been worried."

"I am."

She busies herself with making the coffee and I sit on the barstool and say wearily. "That was quite a scare, but you will be pleased to know Sophia is safe. I can't say she's well but physically I think she's ok."

I see the tears form in the housekeeper's eyes and feel surprised. She obviously cares a great deal for Sophia and she wipes them away before saying huskily, "Will she be coming home?"

"Not just yet. She's staying with some friends to heal. I'm sure she won't be a stranger though; we just have to be patient."

She nods and I can tell she's relieved, and then she says with concern. "And you. This must have come as quite a shock. How are you bearing up?"

"Me?" I stare at her in surprise because of everyone, I'm the least affected but I appreciate her concern and smile my thanks. "You know, Mrs. Billings, this has taught me how much I care for this family. I just want to make sure they are ok and then I'll be happy."

She laughs softly. "They may be a strange bunch but they're family, it counts for a lot."

We share a smile and an understanding. Yes, they may be difficult but they are our kind of complicated and love has a habit of disguising the flaws in people who ordinarily we should run like the wind from. But they are so much more than that. They are made up of many layers and not all of them bad. It's the good in them that creates loyalty and the bad in them that creates a desire to help. I'm not sure I'm up to the job, but I will die trying to make their lives a happier one.

It's not long before Tobias heads into the kitchen looking tired and yet so impossibly hot my mouth waters. He is unshaven, and the dark stubble on his strong jaw arouses the animal in me and his tousled hair makes me itch to run my fingers through it.

Grabbing a coffee from Mrs. Billings, he settles beside me and smiles. "I think that's enough business for one day. I have more important things to occupy my afternoon."

The loaded look he shoots me makes me squirm, and I feel the heat tearing through my body. Mrs. Billings smiles and turns away, and Tobias winks and takes my hand. "Come, we need to be alone."

I almost can't look at Mrs. Billings because his intentions are crystal clear—what must she think?

But she carries on with her chores and as I follow my husband to where I appear happiest, I feel excited for the hours ahead.

CHAPTER 38

TOBIAS

The relief is overwhelming. It's done. Carlos is finally where I want him and Sophia is safe and getting the care she needs. Ana is back by my side, and I can breathe again.

Now I only have one thing in mind and that's carrying on where we left off at the hideaway.

As I pull her in haste after me, she giggles. "Do you always have to move so fast?"

"Not always."

I wink and I see the desire heavy in her eyes.

We reach our bedroom and I say nothing and grind her lips to mine. I want to taste every inch of the beauty I own; mind, body and soul, and I want to make it up to her. Standing back, I say with a wicked glint in my eye, "Get naked."

She blushes and I love the innocence in her as I sit on the bed and watch. Her embarrassment needs to be dealt with because I will not have her feeling uncomfortable around me.

Slowly she edges out of her clothes and I see the desire making her shiver in anticipation. I admire the shapely body of my woman because it's obvious she is all I will ever need or want in life.

Then I stand and approach her and without taking my eyes off her, say thickly, "Undress me."

She swallows hard and yet does my bidding, and the feeling of her light touch makes me hard for her the minute I feel her hands on me.

Soon we are both naked and I say firmly, "Come, we will shower together."

I take her hand and lead her to the bathroom and turn on the warm jets. As the spray hits our bodies, I take the soap and rub it in my hands until the lather forms and then carefully soap her entire body, paying attention to every inch of her perfect skin. She gently moans and I smile. So ready and willing, how I love that sound. As I pay special attention to the place she surrendered to me, she shivers and I whisper, "What do you want, little bird?"

Her eyes open and she looks a little unsure but the intensity of my expression causes her to smile and she says breathlessly, "Fuck me, sir."

She smiles like the innocent with the mouth of a whore, and I love that she has recognized this side of me. Yes, I am one dominant bastard and love a willing woman who likes to play and so I say firmly, "On your knees."

She drops to the floor and I hand her the soap and she takes it and rubs it between the palms of her hand and washes my cock softly and yet with a pressure that makes me even harder. Then I growl, "Show me that you learned the lesson I taught you."

She whimpers and the sound of it causes me great pleasure as she takes my cock in her mouth and sucks it softly at first and then with more pressure. Gently, I rock back and forth and love the sight of her at my feet, on her knees and serving me so obediently. Yes, I knew she was perfect.

The jets of water create even more steam, and I pull her back and up off her feet. Then I kneel before the goddess I love and repay the favor, gently teasing her until she opens up to me like a flower. Her taste is one of pure heaven and I could worship her all day but there is an urgent need in me that I need to address, so I stand and lift her, so her legs wrap around me and hold her hard against the shower wall. Then I kiss that tempting mouth and bite her swollen lips and lose my mind.

She groans against my lips and I growl, "Lesson number five, shower sex."

Then I ease inside her sweet folds and love the way she clenches around my cock and welcomes me in. I rock against her, loving the friction and the warm jets of water that fuel my desire. Her body is slick and wet and slaps against mine as I pin her to the wall. I up my pace and she begins to moan and tremble in my arms and as I pump harder her eyes close and she groans loudly, "Fuck me, Tobias, that feels so good."

"Look at me." I command her and she obeys and her eyes snap open and she stares into mine with a trust mixed with lust, and it drives me crazy. She gasps as I hammer home and as I feel her walls clench around my cock, her screams are loud and music to my ears. She pants and as my wife comes apart around me, I roar like a lion as I shoot my seed and fill her completely.

She slumps against me and I carry her from the shower, grabbing a towel as we pass the heated rail and wrap it around her quivering body. Then I carry her to the enormous bed and lay her gently down before taking my place beside her. As I stroke her hair, I whisper, "I want to renegotiate our contract."

Her eyes snap open in alarm, and I smile. "I want you to cease taking the contraception, we have no use for it."

"You mean…"

I nod. "I want a family, little bird, and I want it with you. I want to see my seed planted in your belly and watch it grow. I want to create a new life and make it a much better one than we both had and I want to do it again and again and again."

"Really?" Her eyes are wide and I kiss her softly on the lips. "And again, and again."

She says in alarm, "Stop, you're scaring me."

I laugh and she leans forward and kisses me softly. "When do we start?"

"Right now."

I kiss her passionately, and she responds immediately.

I feel her hands clawing my back, and it arouses the beast in me. Holding her wrists in one hand, I raise them above her head and growl, "No touching." I love the fact she bites her bottom lip and shivers, and as I begin my explorations, she wiggles underneath me and begins to pant.

I suck each breast, running my tongue around the tip, and she shudders beneath my tongue. Then I burn a trail to her wet and slippery pussy that is throbbing with need. I run my tongue against her clit and she moans and then I gently suck, applying the pressure until she gasps. "I'm going to come."

Immediately, I draw back and growl, "Not until I say so."

Her eyes open and I grin. "I haven't finished with you yet."

Spinning her around until she's on her front, I gently massage her back and love the way her skin feels under my touch. Then I gently nip her neck and kiss every inch of her perfect skin. When I reach her ass, I love the way it stands, pert and full, like a luscious peach ready for the tasting. I take a bite and she groans louder and as I slip my fingers inside her, she bucks against them as I search for her sweetest spot.

The control I have over this woman turns me on and I edge my cock against her crease and she gasps, "Relax, little bird, we have a few more lessons before I go there." I gently rub between her cheeks and my cock throbs hard, desperate for release. Pulling her back so that delectable ass is in the air, I whisper, "I'm going to enter you from behind."

"But…"

"Not there, but it will feel different, tighter, a little painful perhaps. Do you trust me, little bird?"

"Yes." Her voice is husky and so full of need, I smile to myself. Yes, I have many lessons to teach my willing student and so I ease her back onto my cock and groan as she slides onto my shaft like nature intended. As I said, she feels tight and it must burn.

"Does it hurt?"

"A little."

I rock gently back and forth and play with her clit to stimulate her juices, and she groans louder. "That feels so good."

As my balls slap against her ass, I feel the pressure build once more and as she screams louder than before, I shoot hard and fast and groan so loudly they must hear us on the next block.

As our sweat runs and cements us together, I can't ever remember feeling this happy. Maybe there's something in love after all. I know that now I've found it, I will do everything in my power to hold on to it.

CHAPTER 39

TOBIAS

Leaving Ana to sleep, I edge from the bed and shower and dress. There is unfinished business I need to attend to, and if I am to move on with my life, there's one thing that I need to do first.

As usual, Matteo appears as soon as my foot hits the last stair and he nods. "He's waiting for you."

We walk from the house and the car is waiting as I knew it would be and we leave my house behind and head to the farm.

On the way, Matteo brings me up to speed. Todd's family are checked out of hospital and doing well. We sent a car and arranged a first-class flight to take them home. Money has been deposited in their account, meaning they will never worry about it again and the mortgage on their house has been paid off. I have arranged a counselor for them to help them through their dark memories and hope to God those kids grow up with none of the trauma I had to deal with.

All that remains is their father and the man that caused their world to blow apart alongside mine.

By the time we reach the farm, my mind is set. I will do

what's necessary for my family, past and present, and it will be the last time.

We head into the large open space and I see both men tied to chairs, set a little apart from each other.

Two of my enforcers stand behind each one, and a tray of instruments are set up a short distance away.

As I nod, the enforcer behind Todd removes his blindfold and as his eyes adjust to the harsh light directed on him, he starts to shake as he sees my expression.

"Please, tell me, are they safe, my family, please I have to know?"

I nod. "They are."

He breaks down and sobs. "Thank God."

Then I nod to the enforcer behind Carlos and he does the same and Carlos blinks in much the same way and then sneers. "Well, look who finally showed up, the big man himself. You know, I hoped it would be you."

"For what reason?"

"Because I want to see the look in your eye as you do what you are trained to do. You are a fucking cold-blooded killer, and your soul will rot in hell alongside mine. You may hold all the cards in the end but you will have to live with it your whole life."

Taking a chair, I sit astride it and shrug. "Who said I was going to do anything?"

He sneers. "I know you. You slaughtered my family for revenge to repay the favor. Of course, you are going to kill me, I'm the one you hated all along."

"You think? You have a very inflated opinion about your own importance."

Carlos laughs wickedly. "Keep telling yourself that, Tobias. We both know you're loving every minute of this."

I turn to Matteo and say, "Release Todd."

Todd looks wary and says fearfully, "Please, I meant no harm, my family."

"What about your family? Are they more important than mine? Did you think of my poor sister and what she was going to face when you betrayed my family? That is the worst crime of all in my eyes because you chose them over this family and for what? For nothing. They have suffered at his hands and when they were found your kids were so traumatized, they needed hospitalization. Your wife was battered and bloodied and a victim of rape."

Todd's roar of pain drowns out my words and I nod to the enforcer, who grabs him and holds his arms behind his back as I advance toward him and sneer, "You sealed your fate the moment you betrayed me. You should have come to me with this, but you took matters in your own hand. This animal controlled you, and you were like a puppet in his hands. Now you will repay your debt to me and my family."

He begins to shake, and the enforcer drops him to his knees before me and holds his head back, exposing his throat and as I take a knife from the table, I hold it against his skin and the fire in my eyes causes him to cry like a baby as he sobs. "Please, I beg you."

As the blade touches his skin and draws blood, his eyes are wide as I say darkly, "The instrument of death, but whose?"

He looks at me wildly as I turn to Carlos who is trying to look brave, but I can tell by his eyes he sees the madness in mine. "You see, Carlos, I don't consider you worthy of my attention. I slaughtered your family in exchange for mine. I hunted them down and stole from you what they stole from me. An eye for an eye, you know how it goes. But Sophia survived. She was found with just the trauma of what you put her through to live with. You don't deserve to die at my hand because I don't want to see your face when I close my eyes at night. I don't want your death on my conscience because you don't deserve another second of my time and I don't want to even think of you in the future. So, I will allow the man who owes me the most to live with that pain instead of me."

Carlos shouts, "No, I won't be slaughtered by the hired help. I am better than that, I deserve more."

"Only you believe that, Carlos, because you were never the big man you thought you were. You are nothing and always were. Why should I care what you want? It's what *I* want that counts and I want to watch Todd cut you into pieces, before my eyes. Remember, just like you did to my brother. With every slice of that blade, I want to relish your pain. With every drop of blood spilled, I want to watch it fall and remember the blood that was spilled in the name of revenge. I want to bury the past alongside you and walk away from it because I have a future, Carlos, and you do not. Was it all worth it, I doubt it? Is any of this worth a lifetime of pain? No, it's not. So, it ends now and Todd will finish what we started all those years ago because he has a debt to repay and this is how he will pay it."

I turn to Todd and he visibly shakes because he may have worked for my family, but this is a step too far even for him.

I lean toward him and hiss, "Take the knife and do what I ask. Slowly and with menace because you owe it to your family to step up and do what's right. That man terrorized your family and raped your wife. He had them drugged and chained up like animals, and he beat the shit out of her. She was hanging there like a piece of meat and all because you were weak. Don't be that man now and finish the job, so you can face your family and know you revenged them."

He looks at me in astonishment. "You mean, I do this and I'm spared?"

I nod. "You do this and you walk away, your debt repaid.

You will be free to go and never look back because I never want to see your traitorous face again as long as I live."

I hand him the knife and see the resignation in his eyes. Then he turns to Carlos, who shouts, "What the fuck, no, not him. Not a low-life foot soldier, you bastard."

Once again, I take my seat and smile. "I think I'm going to enjoy watching you die, Carlos. It must be a strange feeling, dying alone with no one to mourn the fact you've gone. It must hurt to know you were cut up like an animal and we watched while you screamed through the pain and it must hurt to know you weren't worth my time because you are nothing, Carlos, never were and never will be."

I turn to Todd and say darkly, "Now do it and make sure it's slow and painful."

As I use one man against the other, I make myself watch every flick of that knife. I harden my heart to the sounds of a man dying in the most extreme agony. With every scream and every drop of blood spilled, I think of my family and what they must have suffered that day, and I remember a past I never wanted any part of. It takes Todd fifty minutes to kill Carlos. He retches and passes out several times, and each time the enforcer brings him back to finish the job. Alongside me, Matteo and my other enforcer stand silently watching as the one remaining part of the puzzle completes the picture.

It's over and I am never going back to that dark place in my mind.

As Carlos takes his last breath, Todd falls to his knees and sobs uncontrollably, bathed in the blood of his biggest mistake. I stand and walk away with no more words spoken, because I have none. It's done and there is only one thing left to do.

EPILOGUE

ANASTASIA

I hear Tobias and look up to see him standing in the doorway looking so hot I almost forget we have a job to do.

"Are you done?"

"I think so."

I look at the cases packed up all around me and smile. "How long will we be away?"

"Who knows?"

"Are you sure about this? The house and everything."

He heads toward me and takes me in his arms. "Absolutely."

As he kisses me softly, I feel a sudden burst of love for my husband.

It's been exactly two weeks since we returned from the Reapers and a lot has changed in a very short time.

Today we are heading back to the hideaway and will be there for a while. When we are gone, this house will be knocked to the ground and then work starts on rebuilding it bigger and better and with more of the modern conveniences that make life easier.

OWNING BEAUTY

In the meantime, we are staying at the hideaway and then sailing around the world on the Island Star. Tobias is giving me what I wanted the most and leaving everything behind to take a much-needed vacation.

"How long do you think we'll be away?"

"A year perhaps."

"And you're happy with that?"

"Of course, we need to start our new life, little bird and when we return, it will be to a new beginning and hopefully, we will not be alone."

He rubs my stomach, and I grin. Yes, the pills were banished to the trash and now we just have to wait for nature to take its course. If it happens sooner, we will return and find a temporary home until this one is ready. Then we will begin our life as a family and I can't wait.

"I love you."

I look up at him and stroke his face gently and his hand snaps over mine, holding it there. His eyes soften and he whispers, "I love you too, little bird. You have given me so much—you saved me and I will never stop repaying you for that."

He kisses me softly and then with an urgency that makes me smile. Yes, our trip will have to wait a little longer because we have something much more important to do first.

~

MUCH LATER, we finally step into the middle car for the last time outside this magnificent house. Mrs. Billings steps into the one behind and Matteo takes up his seat in the passenger seat beside the driver. As usual, we travel with quite the entourage and I have grown to accept this is how we must live.

However, Tobias has done the unthinkable and handed over the running of his underground operation to Matteo and is stepping back to take a year off. Sergio Bellini will continue to run his legitimate businesses, and Tobias will be kept updated electronically and via the phone. He has decided to travel with me for a year, and I can't believe he did that for me.

"Have you heard news of Sophia?"

He sighs heavily and settles back in his seat.

"Still the same. She won't leave the Reapers and they are fine with that."

"Do you worry about her?"

He nods. "Of course, but I have to give her some space. She's in the right hands and I know she's safe. When she is ready, I will drop everything to bring her home, whenever that will be."

Reaching for his hand, I squeeze it tightly and rest my head on his shoulder.

We make our way to the airfield and I feel the excitement building. The hideaway. I can't wait to return to a place with so many happy memories. Even the bad ones aren't so bad anymore because I realize they were the catalyst that drove change. I am looking forward to showing my sister and Sebastian my island home when they come for a visit two weeks from now.

Mom is busy searching for husband number two, and Martha is busy keeping her from getting in too much trouble. My biggest regret is that Martha will not join us, and yet I know mom needs her because they have some strange connection that means one cannot exist without the other.

One day I'll discover what that is, but for now, I am just content to head off into the sunset with my husband and live happily ever after.

I hope you enjoyed Owning Beauty. You can read Sophia's story in
Broken Beauty.

"I ran from the beast into the arms of the Devil." *Sophia Moretti*

Maverick
It takes a special kind of glue to mend a broken Angel. She came to the right place—or so she thought.
Broken, traumatized and scared.
Her past was a place that had no business in her future.
But she ran to me. She should have kept running.

Sophia
A man that keeps his secrets hidden behind eyes that are shielded by the blackest shade.
A prince shrouded in the helm of darkness to disguise a heart that is cloaked with the souls of the damned.
A wild Boar dressed in biker leathers, sunglasses and a stinking attitude.
A man who could pick a fight in an empty room.
A God of war.
Just the man I need right now.

As it turns out - I should have kept on running.

If you enjoyed Owning Beauty, please would you be so kind as to leave a review on Amazon?

Join my closed Facebook Group

Stella's Sexy Readers

Follow me on Instagram

Stay healthy and happy and thanks for reading xx

Carry on reading for more Reaper Romances, Mafia Romance & more.
Remember to grab your free copy of The Highest Bidder by visiting stellaandrews.com.

BOOKS BY STELLA ANDREWS

Twisted Reapers

Sealed With a Broken Kiss
Dirty Hero (Snake & Bonnie)
Daddy's Girls (Ryder & Ashton)
Twisted (Sam & Kitty)
The Billion Dollar baby (Tyler & Sydney)
Bodyguard (Jet & Lucy)
Flash (Flash & Jennifer)
Country Girl (Tyson & Sunny)

The Romanos
The Throne of Pain (Lucian & Riley)
The Throne of Hate (Dante & Isabella)
The Throne of Fear (Romeo & Ivy)
Lorenzo's story is in Broken Beauty

Beauty Series
Breaking Beauty (Sebastian & Angel) *
Owning Beauty (Tobias & Anastasia)
Broken Beauty (Maverick & Sophia) *
Completing Beauty – The series

Five Kings
Catch a King (Sawyer & Millie) *
Slade

Steal a King

Break a King

Destroy a King

Marry a King

Baron

Club Mafia

Club Mafia – The Contract

Club Mafia – The Boss

Club Mafia – The Angel

Club Mafia – The Savage

Standalone

The Highest Bidder (Logan & Samantha)

Rocked (Jax & Emily)

Brutally British

Deck the Boss

Reasons to sign up to my mailing list.

- A reminder that you can read my books FREE with Kindle Unlimited.
- Receive a monthly newsletter so you don't miss out on any special offers or new releases.
- Links to follow me on Amazon or social media to be kept up to date with new releases.
- Free books and bonus content.
- Opportunities to read my books before they are even released by joining my team.
- Sneak peeks at new material before anyone else.

stellaandrews.com